14/2
THE ATTACK ON PULWAMA

Vikas Trivedi and Smita Agarwal

Leadstart
INKSTATE

ISBN 978-93-5438-409-7

First published in India 2021 by Inkstate Books
An imprint of Leadstart Publishing Pvt Ltd

Sales Office:
Unit No.25/26, Building No.A/1,
Near Wadala RTO,
Wadala (East), Mumbai – 400037 India
Phone: +91 969933000
Email: info@leadstartcorp.com
www.leadstartcorp.com

Disclaimer: The views expressed in this book are those of the Author and do not pertain to be held by the Publisher.

This is a work of fiction. Names, characters, businesses, places, events, locales, and incidents are either the products of the author's imagination or used in a fictitious manner. Any resemblance to actual persons, living or dead, or actual events is purely coincidental.

Editor: Vaibhav Pathare
Cover: Swapnil Behere
Layouts: Kshitij Dhawale

"What if you were tasked with the protection of the land of your forefathers? What if you were to raid the skies, the land, and the seas for liberation? What if you stepped into the lands of butchers? What if you were killed...only to live?"

*"Some men live and die by themselves; The first kind.
Some do great things to benefit society; the second kind.
Then there are those who seldom dream about being great or selfish altogether. Their only passion- protection and prosperity of their tribe until their last breath; the third kind."*

Dedicated to

To the Brave Indian Army

Acknowledgements

This book has been developed from real incidents and details that are available in the public domain — including print media and TV news channels. It took us two years and a lot of effort to complete the book because of the nature of the content. Apart from background research, we interacted with ex-army personnel, journalists, political analysts, philosophers, political scholars, and the people of Jammu and Kashmir. We offer our sincere appreciation to our friends who explained the ground situation about Jammu and Kashmir.

We cannot express enough thanks to our publisher, editor, designers, and the entire team at Leadstart for their continued support and guidance.

We owe and salute the courage, invaluable service, supreme sacrifices, and determination of our Indian soldiers and their families towards the country.

Jai Hind

Contents

Prologue

The enmity between two men is mortal, between a thousand men is prolonged, and between two nations_- is immortal. And the immortal enmity between the countries is as entangled as the barbed wires that separate them. Picking the right one out of these two is easy, however. It depends upon your orientation of justice & injustice. Such is the paradigm of India & Pakistan, where the former has fought for peace & the latter has waged terror.

The 'Line of Control' keeps their its territories defined. Though, Pakistan's terrorist camps fail to recognize the LoC and operate with their own agenda. The momentary peace is broken between the two countries when an Indian paramilitary convoy in Pulwama is struck with explosives in the homeland. Countless deaths of Indian soldiers lead to anger amongst the citizens, and an NIA investigation ensues.

Long known for its peace policies, diplomatic & servile attitude, India decides to strike back in retaliation. A few weeks after the Pulwama blast, the Indian Air Force calls a stealthy air-strike. In the night's cover, armed with laser-guided bombs & precision targeting systems, a squadron of Indian combat aircraft breach the LoC and level a Pakistani terror campsite with heavy armament. However, as the mission ends, India loses one of its pilots behind the enemy lines.

While no nation questions India's actions, Pakistan labels it as a breach of trust. Indian authorities & Air Force begin contemplating the fate of one of their finest pilots. Security agencies hound for any clue about the status of the Indian pilot. Diplomats invoke their 'full measures' & the tension between the two countries rises to dangerous levels.

Behind the scenes, the NIA Investigator traces tracks of the Pulwama attack & begins unfolding clues leading to a massively destructive conspiracy.

The story grips the reader in a thrilling narrative full of anticipation. The two stories run their course, eventually intersecting at a point that changes the fate of everyone involved. The authors have put in the great effort behind the research, with each element of the narrative fitting itself upon the other to complete the jigsaw!

Overall, an interesting read that would transport the reader straight into the real-world of friends, foes, blood, guns & victory.

War abhors everyone, the right, and the wrong!

Present Day

Hostile F-16 detected, initiating interception, Wing Commander Anand Varthaman radioed the ground station. "Go ahead, keep us updated" Ground Control affirmed. A peaceful routine air patrol by the Indian Air Force had just hit a twist. They've been expecting notorious neighbor's eyes into the Indian borders one of these days. Pakistan had made a desperate attempt too soon.

30,000 feet above the ground, inside the cockpit, sat one of the most highly skilled pilots, Wg. Cdr. Anand Varthaman. He is an ace pilot, a married man, son of an Ex-Air Force maven, and a patriot who had never in his career let an enemy intrusion by air into the Indian sub-continent. In his squadron, Anand and his Mig-'Striker'-21 were jokingly called invincible. Though, the time was insisting too much on testing this man-machine duo's invincibility. The day had a different plan altogether.

Anand pursued the F-16 for a few minutes. This aircraft had Pakistan Air Force markings on the tail and had made a few passes over the Indian border. "You are flying in an unauthorized airspace," Anand established radio contact with the enemy aircraft. "Identify yourself and state your intentions," he sent a clear message to avoid a wrong shootout. "State your intentions or you will be shot down, you are flying in the Indian air space," his voice penetrated the F-16's cockpit through the radio.

The two combat birds were hardly flying a mile-and-a-half apart, at an astonishing speed of Mach 1. Pakistani F-16 did not respond. It kept flying towards the enemy border as if trying to evade the air pursuit. "Command, enemy aircraft is not responding. Request permission to engage, over!" Anand requested the command center. However tempting the target looked, Wg. Cdr. Anand couldn't have shot it down. He knew about the complexities of international relations and the misunderstanding a wrong move could cause. His engagement of the F-16 could even trigger a war between the two Asian neighbors. The time to decide, right or wrong, was slipping by. Anand was concerned about the intel that the Pakistan jet might have gathered, or it could be a distraction. Pakistan's notorious activities could be smelled miles away by the war veterans of India.

Back in the IAF Command Center, Air Vice Marshal entered the Control Room. "Sir," Group Captain Rohan Brar saluted the AVM before he briefed him about the escalating situation. "Who is flying the Indian jet?" AVM asked Grp. Cpt. Brar. "Anand Varthaman, sir," he replied. "Hm. Tell Anand it is his call" and the AVM left the control room. Rohan immediately grabbed the radio headset and relayed the message to Anand, who now had flown miles in pursuit of the F-16. "Hawk 1, Hawk 1, your call!" and Anand had a little smile on his face. "Acknowledged. I am taking down this bastard," the last ever message Anand relayed from the cockpit that day.

A *few Moments Later*

"Waseem, Waseem, I am going down, Ya Allah!" Distressed screams of a person over the radio panicked everyone in the Pakistan Air Force Control room. "What is happening?" Pak Air Command Chief Firoz Yahiya ground his teeth at the fellow subordinates. "Janab….Janab our jet is down. We've…lost contact with Flying Officer Armaan," Captain Waseem said to Yahiya, anticipating an unpredictable reaction from him. Yahiya didn't flinch. He stood at ease, took a deep breath, and took out a cigar. Before lighting it, he asked Waseem, "Is he alive…Armaan?" "We have sent a recovery convoy to the location. We expect the debris to be inside a few kilometers of our border," said Capt. Waseem. The smoke from the cigar spread across the radar screens as a red dot blinked on the map.

A Few Kilometers inside Pakistan's LoC

A boy in his early teens walks down the uneven dusty road. He seems oblivious to the world, swinging an arm-long stick, taking notice of his sheep and goats every few minutes. He continues to walk in his tattered clothes and foot-biting shoes when a loud bang scares him and his flock. The boy turns around and shouts, "Abba, Salim, Abba, Abba…" and runs away as his eyes witness a horrific blast followed by a cloud of smoke rising towards the sky.

The vicinity sees moments of panic and confusion, and in no time, a group of locals shows up following the boy's foot trail. They all seem to be indistinguishable from each other, wearing clothes of a similar nature, having similar reactions, and continuously pointing towards the blast site. "Salim, look at that," the flock rearing boy grabs his elder brother's attention to point out a large white cloth fluttering over the bushes some few hundred feet from the crowd. "What is that *bhaijaan?*" he asks while herding his scared sheep together. Saleem, his elder brother, looks up to the sky, then towards the fluttering cloth, and grabs a stone.

The crowd is villagers living inside Pakistan's side of the LoC. Their murmuring grows as they slowly advance towards the rising flames. The group's behavior was primitive, and it was almost as if an 'extraordinary' event had occurred.

Meanwhile, the two brothers got near their point of interest. "What is this *bhaijaan*" the little one asked the elder brother again. Saleem was less than interested in his brother's query. He crouched and moved towards the large cloth through which many nylon ropes were oozing out entangled. Saleem looked at the boy with a smirk because he knew what was lying ahead of them. "It is a parachute, people fly in this," he said. "Like a kite?" the little shepherd grew curious. Saleem took the little shepherd's stick and began poking the parachute's fabric lightly. No movement ensued. He then took the stone in his right hand, threw it with all the might on the parachute, and ran back. A close inspection by them revealed faint groans coming from under the parachute, from inside the thick bushes.

It was a matter of seconds when the crowd gathered around the parachute as the shepherd brothers alarmed everyone. Waking up to a crowd of illiterate and primitive humans, with sticks and stones in their hands, can be one of the most terrifying feelings for anyone. And, whoever was under that parachute, had clearly intruded these people's territory.

The fire melted the remains of the aircraft. The pilot had ejected on time. Here he was now, on the ground, in terrible shape, and scared. His life threw him another distress, and this one was even harder to escape. The man sadly woke up after a few wooden sticks hit him. His breaths were deep, his body was exuding sweat and blood, and his mind wasn't able to process the situation he was in.

People were looking at him like apes in a group, trying to decipher where and why he'd landed from the sky. As the pilot regained control of his senses, his mouth spurt blood, and a blood-curdling scream ensued as his right leg broke. "*Shaitaan, Shaitaan, kaafir*" they shouted unanimously. Some took stones no less heavy than a brick, some had farming tools forged locally. The pilot who fell from the sky was being lynched. Some said to flay his skin, some suggested burning him alive. The innocent- villagers were revealing their dark side cumulatively. It was ugly, horrible, and worthy of derision in every manner.

Mankind, for a moment, proved that it is very well capable of becoming evil and God at will, only it chooses evil every time and limits God to society's imagination. Saleem and his younger brother saw everything with their eyes wide open. Saleem, now 16, was expected to be a 'man,' as per the customs of his village. And maybe it was his desperation to achieve manhood that he threw a stone with all his might which hit his forehead making a deep cut. His body lied there as the tribe of people looted his blood-stained belongings. A radio, a 9 mm Glock, and a few cigars were enough to celebrate their 'kill.'

A few hundred feet away from the lynching spot, from behind a lush green but lonely Weeping Willow, Anand saw the horror as it began.

He knew the enemy well, yet never expected this side of them. These were just the villagers. 'They probably will kill him thinking he is an Indian,' Indian Wg. Cdr. thought to himself. Though moved by the intensity and gravity of the danger he was in, Anand refused to lose his cool.

It was a relief as the villagers had no idea of 'another' pilot in the vicinity.

Anand radioed in the Indian Air Force base station at minimum volume. "Hawk 1" is down, I am still in action. An anti-aircraft gun took me down," he said, For now, all he needed was to stay low behind the giant willow tree and think of a way out to survive. 'I just hope Pakis did not intercept my radio message,' he thought to himself. He had no other option, however.

Anand took out a small tactical briefcase, small but fat, and put his combat pilot mind to use. He opened the case with a click and retrieved his M9, a reliable weapon capable of instilling confidence in him at this moment. He loaded it with a 15-round magazine, holstered it, and spread out the map. There was also a small booklet whose cover read 'Land Survivor Handbook for Air Force Pilots.'

The case had a knife, a lighter, and a few high calory eatables. Anand took a peek behind the willow to see the group gone farther away, shouting and aimlessly firing the dead pilot's pistol.

He sat down and opened up a bar of chocolate. Anand's body was in a state of mild shock as it had suffered great stress and impact during the ejection. Thankfully, his Martin-Baker ejection seat put him down on land, alive. Despite the intense pressure on the mind and body, Anand chose chocolate, cigarette, and cool over panic. As he chewed the chocolate and smoked the cigarette, he spread out a map and some mission documents. Anand wanted to narrow down the viable location of his aircraft. In his ejection seat was a powerful beacon through which he could contact Indian forces without being traced. 'It must be a few miles south of this place,' he thought while triangulating a location on the map.

Suddenly, Anand was startled by something in front of him. A pair of legs, hairy and of a brown-white color streak. It was a goat. A sigh of relief followed, though only for a few seconds before Anand noticed two human eyes staring at him from some twenty feet away from the goat. Saleem's younger brother saw Anand in his uniform. He appeared something similar to the 'last' one, something dangerous yet benign, with no facial expression, Anand slowly stood up against Willow's trunk.

Having been a student in different Central Schools/KendriyaVidyalayas, Anand acquired the skills to adjust to and fit into new surroundings comparatively quickly. He was mostly an extrovert and developed new friendships quickly and was part of cricket and football teams through much of his school life.

He tried to minimize his body movements to not frighten the child and reached for his M9. "What is your name, kid?" asked Anand without advancing towards him. Some 50 goats now surrounded the duo. "Do you like chocolates?" he threw one at the kid. The child picked it up and smiled. His uneven and missing teeth shone in the sun. What a relief it was for Anand.

A little far from the willow, a crosshair had Anand in its line of fire, and a cunning eye desperate to kill. The eye could see the Indian pilot and kid exchanging some things and getting along. Wing Commander Anand had taken control of the situation, and he began packing his tactical survival kit. "So how far is the lake, Rehman?" he asked his new friend. "Not much. We can get there in a few minutes if we walk," said Rehman as he feasted upon the nut-ridden chocolate bar. Suddenly a villager aims for Anand's head.

He ducked with Rehman and reached for his M9. He hurriedly radioed in, "I am compromised. I have been spotted by the enemy." I am moving south of my current location towards the jet. Trace me through this part if you can. Anand asked the little dude to run away, and he did. There was no point in wasting bullets in a blind fight. Anand had limited ammunition, which he deemed necessary as the 'last resort' in close-quarter combat.

He ran and ran. Though his body wasn't allowing him, he was short of breath, trying hard to focus, and barely managing to run at a constant pace. The human body has a limit. Anand had to stop for some glucose to energize and water to quench his thirst behind the enemy lines. The lake was nowhere to be seen. He scanned behind his left shoulder, then the right one. No movement. Nothing. He found himself in the cover of some trees, not dense, but fairly fine to cover him.

He slept, inviting some major decisions of his life to pour in as he tried to calm his body and mind. Like fellow kids, he dreamt of becoming a cricketer during his tender age. He thought it would be cool to open the batting for the Indian cricket team and enjoyed watching his cricketing idols on TV. But, the idea of being a hero to millions of kids all across India and beyond – how can that *not* appeal to an adolescent? Such thoughts poured and allowed him a nap, which was shortened by an interruption

Call it fate, god's plan, karma, or randomness of the universe that Anand woke up after falling asleep surrounded by the villagers. Same faces, the same anger, same tools, and the same intentions. For a brief moment, the courageous Indian pilot thought it was over. His killer instinct drove him towards his holster, which was now empty. Anand was surrounded, weaponless, and at the mercy of primitive forces that couldn't tell an apple from orange but could very well butcher a human being. The distinct 'IAF' patch on his shoulder stood out, and Anand closed his eyes as attempting to escape wasn't even worth trying. He felt to remember his father, a former officer in the IAF. Due to him, Anand had absorbed a lot of stuff about what it meant to be an officer in the Indian armed forces and what kind of life that entailed – the joys to be savored as well as the sacrifices that need to be made.

A few well-muscled men, the butchers of the villager, grabbed him by the neck and beat him black and blue. Anand blacked out in his right eye. His brain became numb. A few hits on his right leg severely damaged it, probably broke it. He cried in agony, yet held his vulnerability back in front of the skin-flaying crowd. By now, his face was brimming with fresh blood, his belongings were looted and his final countdown was about to begin.

As the sun was about to set, upset from everything humankind did to each other and the planet, aerial shots fired from the assault rifles at a distance stopped the procession. A few jeeps, an armored vehicle, and a few foot soldiers arrived at the spot. "Leave the man alone!" An officer of the Pakistani armed forces commanded. The crowd was uncivilized, stubborn, and aggressive. They launched a few aggressive moves at Anand, refusing to hand him over to the Pak defence forces. They wanted to burn Wg. Cdr. Anand alive. Though, assault rifles have always successfully changed minds whenever required.

Balakot Air Strike by the IAF and the Indian Government

Since a few days...

When the Pulwama attacks happened, the armed forces went into a heightened state of alert. They expected that the political leadership will give them the requisite permission to inflict a proportionate amount of damage on Pakistan in retaliation. That the Air Force would play a role was not a given but the IAF nevertheless had war-gamed what kind of retaliations it could carry out.

These war plans had been built upon India's experience in the 1971 war as also the Kargil War. Operation Safed Sagar had been a success even though Pakistan committed war crimes by torturing a pilot who was captured.

IAF had been constrained in that war to fly within the LoC. The Mirage-2000H had proven itself with its capability to deliver precision-guided munitions.

The political leadership met after the Pulwama attacks. The Cabinet Committee on Security invited the three service chiefs to the meeting. The Cabinet Secretariat had asked the Chiefs to come prepared with the top-secret war plans.

The Cabinet was presented with various options. An airstrike on terrorist training camps in Balakot was considered the best option as it involved the least amount of civilian damage.

The Cabinet green-lighted the bombing of the terrorist training camps. The Air Force was given a free hand to plan the operation within the next few weeks. The service chiefs met daily to plan the strikes and any possible responses by Pakistan.

The chiefs were shown satellite imagery of the Balakot camps. India's technical intelligence gathering agency had tapped into the cellphone network in the Balakot region and concluded that there were several hundred terrorists 'trainees' living in the camps there.

Everyone agreed that this was a legitimate military target. The details of the bombing mission were discussed. This was going to be an unprecedented air raid deep inside Pakistan's borders – something that had not happened since 1971.

Weapons and delivery platforms were analyzed. India's precision-guided munitions options had expanded since the Kargil War. The upgraded Mirages and Jaguars offered choices as to the choice of delivery platforms. AWACS platforms and aerial refueling capability added a range of options to complicate things to confuse the enemy.

It was decided that fighter aircrafts would scramble from frontline airbases in Punjab to confuse Pakistan's military planners. The actual Balakot bombing would be carried out by bombers that would take off from the hinterland.

A date was agreed upon. Things were kept on an even keel to

make sure Pakistan did not suspect anything was going to happen on the night of February 26. Even the retirement ceremony of the retiring chief of Western Air Command went ahead as planned.

As the day turned into evening and then night, fighters scrambled from about ten airbases. This was a complex operation involving thousands of airmen. The decoy fighters turned towards Barmer and then turned towards Pakistan before returning. The main attack aircraft comprising the Mirage-2000s scrambled from Gwarlior and quickly entered into Pakistan easily evading Pakistan's radars and air defence.

This was facilitated by the availability of AWACs high in the air. In just a few minutes Balakot came within striking range and the Mirage pilots released their precision-guided munitions. Then they turned towards India and left Pakistan airspace even as Pakistan scrambled its F-16s. India's air warriors were safely home before Pakistan could do anything about it.

The next day, Pakistan was the first to publicly declare that India had attacked it. Pakistan claimed that India had tried to intrude into its airspace but that Pakistan's fighters had rebuffed India's attempts. Pakistan claimed that the Indian fighter pilots had to drop their munitions in a hurry and caused no damage to Pakistan.

India also officially announced the airstrikes and announced that terrorist training camps had been targeted and successfully destroyed in Balakot.

The next day, Pakistan sought to respond to the humiliation from India by launching F-16s towards India. Indian pilots, including Anand were more than ready and they engaged the Pakistani F-16s.

When someone chooses to be an air force pilot in India, they make the choice knowing full well the inherent dangers. Or, at least, they should know about all the dangers and then make an informed decision.

Anand had been observing the material gains and a safe job from many people across the environment. People had shifted to "greener pastures"- From London to Houston to Silicon Valley. While the young Anand found lots to like about his life in the armed services, working as an officer and spending one's working life dealing with various challenges of the job.

When the time came for him to appear for the inevitable entrance exams, he cleared the NDA exam and became a gentleman cadet at the Academy.

His three years at the Academy were a time of both physical and intellectual growth for him as he learned fundamental physics and engineering mathematics concepts. His time went on trying to understand electronics concepts such as semiconductors and how they work. He loved everything about electronics – both the theory part and the practical part. He learned about various electronic circuits, gates, and digital signal processing.

After finishing NDA, he joined the Air Force Academy. As a flying cadet, he learned about the Principles of Aircraft Control – about rudders and ailerons and wind shear and much else.

He started training on gliders – first with a trainer onboard and then flying solo. After finishing his one-year training at the Academy, he was commissioned into the Air Force as a flying officer.

His first posting was at Halwara Air Force Station.

Anand was assigned to first fly MiG-21s initially. Anand knew that this was a stepping stone to Sukhois. Mastering the MiG-21 was quite challenging. Anand had a busy schedule of classroom training by flight instructors combined with daily sorties in the MiG-21s.

Fighters fly fast but run out of fuel in an hour – unless refueled. Keeping these in view, Anand's MiG-21 training consisted of learning how to engage enemy aircraft in air-to-air combat.

Price of any war: Pain

14 Days Earlier

Clinton Joseph, Lead Investigation Officer of the National Investigation Agency, was a man of rationale, logic, and facts. He was the kind that people would look up to for justice, for he was unbiased and had mastered his emotions. Mr. Joseph, throughout a brilliant career, had solved multiple cases that were deemed impossible by ordinary minds. His specialty, though, was investigating acts of terror and the minds behind them.

It was a pleasant morning in Srinagar, living heaven on Earth, and Clinton Joseph was enjoying his morning tea in his Government Bungalow's lush green garden. Acres of vast mountains stretch, birds soaring to remind the earthlings of the freedom beyond, crystal clear rills quenching the land's thirst with fresh water, and nature's very own scent in the air together worked in symphony to make the cold-hearts melt.

Joseph wasn't a romantic at heart though, neither was he a poet. His hobbies included playing chess, shooting cardboard targets with rifles, and training dogs. He was a divorcee for 5 years now, vowed never to love again. Though, he kept lying to himself. For he fell in love with this scenic Indian town long ago!

This day was different. As soon as he finished his coffee and recalled his meeting with the Chief Secretary of Defense in New Delhi, his cell phone rang. "Hello, Jai Hind, sir," he said. "Jai Hind, Joseph. Listen to me. We have a Red Alert situation in the ministry. Report immediately," the man on the phone said. "At once, sir," Clinton replied. "Get to PULWAMA ASAP! There is a chopper at the Srinagar airport. Meet the Assistant Commandant of CRPF once you reach," the voice articulated each word crisply. "What is it, sir?" "44 CRPF souls killed in action. We smell terrorist play. Update me once you get there." As the voice hung up the phone from the other side, Clinton kept his cell phone in the pocket, slid out a pack of Dunhill Cigarettes, and lit one as if he needed one.

"Powell Ji, get the car ready, we are leaving for the airport," Joseph said as he rushed inside the bungalow remembering something. He found himself in his room, which inhabited a small but heavy metal safe. 8 Ticks of the buttons on the number pad and the safe threw itself open. Clinton took out a black pouch, threw it on the bed, but not before taking out a small piece of paper. Clinton held the small piece of paper in front of himself while gazing at it like a puzzled man. They were mere words, and some numbers written in that paper. A statement was given to the NIA by a suspect a few years back. This little piece of paper had it.

Clinton hustled with his briefcase, strapped his steel wristwatch on his right hand, grabbed his issued pistol, his notepad, and memo, and left for Srinagar airport in an old but well-maintained white HM Ambassador.

It was barely over an hour when a white Beechcraft King Air 350 touched down on the tarmac of a small airstrip in Pulwama.

The door unfolded and transformed into the stairs on which Joseph climbed down with 3 of his selected Investigation Officers. "Jai Hind, sir," a tall, well-built man in camouflaged paramilitary uniform greeted the NIA gentlemen. "Jai Hind, Mr. Shikara," Clinton shook his hands firmly. Ram Shikara was the Assistant Commandant of the CRPF battalion stationed at the Pulwama, the first responders to the gruesome and cowardly attack. Shikara lead the NIA team out of the airport. "When did it happen?" Clinton asked "4 Hours, sir," he said with a weird hesitation in his voice. "What happened officer, you fine?" Clinton asked the man firmly as he put on his sunshades. Shikara hesitated. And the troop left for the attack site in an armoured anti-riots vehicle.

As the car sped through the deserted roads closed for the civilian traffic, Clinton had only the image of that little paper in his mind. *'We made a mistake,'* he confessed something to himself, and the vehicle soon stopped at the side of the road. The scene was chaotic. There was smoke, there were black pieces of burnt metal, people were surrounding the area, and paramilitary troops were trying to restore peace in this small universe that had just been shaken out of its existence.

The investigators deboarded the vehicle. Clinton slowly took-off his shades, his mouth paralyzed from the awe, eyes filled with sorrow, and body locked into the rage instinct. For a few seconds, the world did not exist for him. "Holy s**t," Praveen, an accompanying investigator, said without regard for any formality. This was no time for rules, obligations, and formalities. Anyone within a few hundred meters of the vicinity was dead or floating in a swirl of complex yet highly intense emotions.

Clinton took a few steps forward and began examining each yard, each burnt piece. He tried to recall a memory worse than this, perhaps more blood spilled than this to console himself. No luck did he get from his memory palace. Clinton Joseph began interviewing the people around. His way of investigation involved re-creating the story of the incident, connected with the nexus of causality, and ultimately leading to the point in time where he was present.

He scanned the scene around him and intuitively re-constructed what happened in his mind.

'The sky was yellow. Traffic was less on the roads. These roads awaited the CRPF Jawans who were stranded in Jammu since the 4th of February due to snow-blocked roads.'

"Sir, the convoy shredded 16 vehicles at Qazigund. It is approximately 90 minutes from here. 16 more armoured vehicles joined the CRPF convoy from there," personnel said to Clinton.

The young man's voice played back at the back of Clinton's mind while he recreated the agonizing scene in his mind. It was his favourite thing to do. To complete the puzzle and get the story straight.

'The convoy was probably traveling at a nominal speed. A normal thing to do when escort vehicles are clearing the way. Right, escort vehicles, where were they?' Clinton Joseph stumbled across a question.

"Where were the escort vehicles? I would like to have a word with the officers in them," he said to Shikara with no evidence of the disgust in his voice following the scene of the blast. Clinton took a few steps forward, lit another cigarette. But this time his hands trembled as he positioned the lighter's flame in front of his nose.

Joseph was being internally agitated. Though he was a tough man who was used to seeing blood, it was not the bloodshed that made his soul die a little inside, but the sheer magnitude of the destruction and the backstories of Jawans that disturbed his conscious waking self. *'They were returning for deployment. From their homes. Did they know it was their last time on earth? That it was the last time they ever saw their loved ones?'* he talked to himself inside the head. And every time he talked to himself, he seemed to be punishing himself with the burden of some hidden blame.

The scene he next saw probably struck him the hardest. There stood the bus which took a direct hit from a speeding vehicle. *'They had loaded the SUV with explosives. It sped, overtook other vehicles in the convoy, and converged itself into the bus,'* he thought. There laid the vehicle, a bus in service of the CRPF for years. Now turned into a piece of a metal ball, so badly disfigured that it would be impossible for any man to do it on purpose. *'It was a bus that turned into a hearse. RDX. No other explosive can turn a big vehicle into scrap.'*

Clinton went close to the point of impact. An officer followed him to assist his actions amidst the darkest and sad site Clinton had ever seen. Blood spatters and brain matter splashed on the electric poles, chunks of half-cooked human flesh lying on the road. Nothing was recognizable. Blood was all fresh as if the killings just happened minutes ago. Both the men put on a small cloth to spare their senses of the smell of burnt human flesh mixed with molten metal.

Clinton's eye got fixed on something. It was a small tricolour patch woven over a cloth, the cloth placed over the hand, and the hand separated from the rest of the body.

"This is the exact spot of the blast, sir," the assisting officer informed him. "Lab has found the traces of RDX."

"Any information on the *Fidayeen?*" he asked. "Two men in an SUV. That is all we know," the young man replied.

Clinton shook his head subtly. "Connect me to the home ministry," he said as he fled towards the vehicle for some water.

A Warrior's Story

Anand was not a particularly philosophical kind of person. Nor was he the kind of person who needed specs because of too much time spent burrowing inside books. Yet, he did take an interest in the history of wars and warfare. He read a little bit about the greats of our country's recent history since independence – Air Marshal Arjan Singh and Field Marshal Manekshaw. General Sundarji was known as a great scholar and strategist who wrote the book on how to do force projection on our neighbour or how to intimidate it using the superiority of our conventional forces.

Anand lived a hectic life full of flight training and other regular activities. Holidays were rare but when he did go on those rare vacation trips, his thoughts turned towards finding a girl with whom he could share his thoughts and feelings. His parents cleverly arranged some match-ups while he was home in Chennai on vacation from the Air Force. Anand took some potential life partners out for coffee. These never went too far as the girls were mostly into the IT sector. Anand thought of the plenty of doctor couples and IAS couples and then he thought it would be a good idea to find a life partner who was also in the armed forces as that would mean both would share some level of commitment to work and also have an implicit understanding of what it takes to be an officer in the Indian Armed services. Every profession has a certain 'culture' – whether it's the medical profession or aviation or armed forces and so forth. You can only understand the culture when you live it.

Luckily, by the time Anand became a flying officer, the IAF was admitting women into various branches of the Air Force – some were even helicopter pilots though none had yet been permitted to fly in combat situations. Anand's path crossed with some female IAF helicopter pilots.

He first got talking with Nandini, a helicopter pilot, during the IAF Day celebrations in Tambaram. Over drinks, the two pilots had a 'professional' exchange of ideas regarding flying. They exchanged phone numbers and promised each other to keep in touch. Anand got a positive first impression of her.

In subsequent meetings at the Officer's Club, both took things further by discussing their family and educational backgrounds. They had a shared interest in Tamil songs and Hollywood movies. Both realized that they found each other to be comfortable together.

Anand wondered whether to broach the tough topics before marriage or afterward – dying, getting captured by the enemy, acquiring some permanent injury in some accident, and other unknowable parts of an aviator's life.

While he was wondering when to take the next step and start discussing marriage, the Mumbai attacks happened. That altered the course of his life as the terrorist attacks made it plain to both of them about the unpredictability and fleeting nature of life.

Anand was a rookie Sukhoi-30MKI pilot based out of Punjab. When the attacks started on the evening of November 26, 2008, he was having a drink at the Officer's Club. All the pilots were asked to be ready to scramble with 15 minutes' notice. So, he spent the next four days more or less in his flight suit.

He followed the developments in Mumbai on TV and some

of his pilot colleagues were chomping at the bit wanting to bomb Pakistan but Anand was mature enough to realize that the orders and decisions for attacks or war were to come and be made by his superiors and civilian authorities. He was relieved that all-out war did not break out between India and Pakistan.

Later on, when things cooled down between India and Pakistan and Anand got a brief opportunity to visit Chennai, he arranged to have coffee with Nandini. Anand maintained a serious composure during the coffee. Both were meeting each other in person after several months. Both went through a few tough months professionally on account of the Mumbai attacks. They both appeared to have aged prematurely.

After they went through a standard chat updating each other about the well-being of their folks, there was silence between them. Anand was determined to raise the topic of marriage today. Nandini wondered whether Anand was going to talk about marriage or not.

"So, what now?" Anand began.

"Yes?" Nandini looked at him quizzically with raised eyebrows.

"I mean, what do we do in three months from now, six months, three years … time flies."

"Hmmm."

"Have you thought about marriage?" Anand asked with increased heartbeats.

She kept silent. Anand got scared as hell.

After an interregnum that appeared to stretch forever to him, she responded: "Yes. I think it's time to get married."

Anand was overjoyed. But … wait … she said 'time to get married' but didn't say 'time for us to get married.'

This raised the stakes even higher for him – was there someone else? Could she be calling all this off? What the … Anand was about to faint as he could barely breathe – it was as if someone had put a heavy load on his chest.

After mentally framing a few alternative ways to ask the question, Anand finally went with: "You have someone in mind?"

She smiled ever so slightly.

The wait was killing Anand.

She thought to respond with: "Duffer. I am talking about 'our' marriage."

But she went with: "What about you?"

Anand thought about saying "we can get married" or "let us get married" or "I am ready to marry you" but he finally went with: "What about us?"

She smiled a little more and pushed a few strands of hair from across her face.

Anand was unsure whether that gesture should increase his confidence level or sink it further.

"You tell."

"We can get married … tomorrow if you want." Anand blurted out.

She laughed out loud.

Anand was worried but also relieved that it was now finally out in the open. A decision will be made finally one way or the other.

"So?" Anand asked after a while.

She thought about how to reply for a while and finally said: "Yeah, let us get married."

She tried to keep her excitement under tight control as she said this since she was herself breathing quite fast and she wanted to hide this fact from Anand.

It was as if a heavy burden had been lifted and both could breathe freely now. Both kept silent and let their heartbeats become normal again.

The dates for marriage were fixed and nothing happened on the India-Pakistan front to play spoilsport in their plans. If anything, the Miracle on The Hudson happened a month before they got married. A good omen if you were into those sorts of things. They discussed it on the phone and admired the courage of Captain Sully Sullenberger. They had already discussed and compared the career of — and the life as — a commercial airline pilot versus that of a pilot in the Air Force. They were on the same page about their choices to be in the armed forces.

Paul Kalanithi's memoir When Breath Becomes Air had come out recently and Anand had heard about the book. He carried that book among others and managed to read the slim book and was quite moved and stunned by Kalanithi's life story. How can you reach the pinnacle of your career, be in your mid-to-late thirties, and then get told that it was now time for you to say goodbye to it all, to your wife, to your profession, to life itself? They were practically the same age – Kalanithi and Anand.

But that's what happened with Dr. Kalanithi. Anand thought that at least with pilots, even if the worst comes to pass, they will be dead in a second or at least die quickly. Cancer stretching across years is a cruel way to die. He wondered how he would react to such a diagnosis.

They discussed this, Anand and Nandini, about life, death, and much else...

Freedom is not free

A windowless room with stale air, chair kept in the middle, a weak light bulb burning with its insufficient might in the corner, and a man sitting on the chair. His hands tied with great care; his eyes blindfolded. The man's heavy head lies lifeless on his right shoulder, and he seems to be barely breathing. Anand was behind the enemy lines in the most vulnerable state. Back there in India, he did not know for sure what was happening. Though Anand cared about the Indian government's activities, but not because of rescue being his top priority, because of the 'mission sensitive' information that could lead to 'instability' of the relations between the two countries.

Anand had his thoughts, opinions on the war. These started pouring back in while he was already in the injured state. He believed that in war, military men will die on both sides who are professional soldiers with families. War can lead to the deaths of thousands and that means thousands of families will be in mourning. What will be the result of a war with such loss of life? Probably nothing.

Anand had always felt it curious– to reflect about how the

nature of war or fighting had shifted over the centuries – for several thousand years, fighting involved actual hand to hand combat; you had to kill your opponent with your own hands, most likely by using either a sword or a spear. Cavalry soldiers were the … shall we say … the 'top guns' of their day, Anand remembered with a little smile, as he was adjusting to his pain. Then gunpowder and dynamite were invented and came into play. Eventually, aircraft was invented and quickly used in war. You could drop bombs on soldiers and civilians from several kilometers away. You could randomly maim and kill an unknown number of people from several kilometers up in the air. It probably caused less trauma for the men of the bomber squadrons in the Second World War as they didn't have to kill all the women and children with machetes. The effect and result though remained the same. And what were the results of such a conflagration? The countries exist which existed before. The only difference being that the victors got to make and keep nukes while the vanquished were denied access to nukes. German and Japanese cities were summarily destroyed using conventional bombs dropped from the air and their civilians suffered immensely. There is no real accounting of how many babies got burned to death in those fire bombings though the death toll in the Second World War is estimated to vary between 50 million to 100 million.

One death is a tragedy; a million deaths is a statistic.

Anand was preparing his mind and body for what he expected to come. The chair he was sitting on was no less than the execution chair. He was well aware of the danger he was in. All those stories of the prisoners of war in the Pakistani cells were potent enough to make anyone choose an easy death over what the Pakistani army inflicted upon the captured personnel. So, Anand recalled his 'torture' training, something he learned during an international joint-military exercise a few years back.

"It is going to be like hell, but real, very real," Col. Brook of the U.S Marines instructed a mix of Indian and American ace pilots. *"Soft nations adhere to Geneva convention. Fanatic and extremist nations don't,"* he continued. *"If an extremist enemy captures you alive and rescue is a long way, you will have only two options. First, find a way to escape. You must be quick in doing this. Quick in thinking and quick in taking action. Second, kill yourself." "Nobody would blame you for committing suicide. It will be a far noble choice than enduring the pain and then dying in the ungodly enemy territory,"* Col. Brook's eyes burnt bright with rage.

"I have seen the enemy doing inhumane and brutal things to the prisoners without flinching. Burning the skin with hot tongs, flaying the inner thigh skin with rough blades, clipping the tongue with gardening tools, gouging the eyes while the person is still alive, electrocution, uprooting the fingernails, breaking the knee caps with a hammer, raping, drowning, or being fed to hungry dogs." Brook's word picture of the real-world torture sent chills down the spines of everyone that listened.

"Though, it all goes away. The pain, the fear, and the anxiety of being captured by the enemy. Once you accept the idea, you'll be comfortable dealing with the sadistic side of the enemy. Your mind will be the key factor in ensuring your survival, even with the worst odds. I'd strongly advise you to not take your own life if, God forbid, the enemy captures you. All I ask you is a favour. I ask you to identify your primal self, your killer instinct. Once your mind gets locked into that mode, trust me, you can pave your way back amidst a thousand enemies."

Those words, the training, Col. Brook's face, all manifested in Anand's mind. He prepared himself for the worst. However, fear couldn't paralyze him and his mind began scanning for a window of opportunity to escape.

The heavy steel gate moved, metal clung, and creaks prevailed. Two guards stationed outside of Anand's cell had to lead someone in. Anand knew the time had arrived. The time when the enemy will ask him questions, and he will have to answer.

The man stood up like a mountain in front of Anand, lit a cigar, and put the shining metal lighter in his pocket. "You want a cigar?" the man asked him. Anand 'looked' toward the sound through his blindfold. His nose could sense the smoky blowout from the man's cigar. Anand preferred to not respond to the man's offer. "A coffee perhaps?" the man offered him again. "I am fine," said Anand as he looked away. His voice had a strange reflection of his inner strength, which was intimidating to the man with the cigar. "I am Firoz Yahiya, Commander of the Pakistani Air Force," the man introduced himself. "Did you know you were in Pakistan?" he asked. Anand acted as if he did not heed. He didn't respond to any of his words.

Yahiya took a big puff from his Black Cuban Cigar, "You don't speak?" Silence still ensued after this question. "Haha! You're good, officer. You're good. Your country has taught you not to talk to the 'strangers' I bet! Good. I appreciate that" he said in the most sarcastic tone ever. Anand was realizing the tremendous anger buried deep inside Firoz Yahiya's mind. His choice of words, style of persuasion, and direct approach to him spoke volumes about the man to him. He just had no idea about what Yahiya would do in case he chose not to speak. And he got his answer soon. "You know we have 'specialists' who can make people speak anything, do anything, confess anything," Yahiya spoke. Meanwhile, two guards came and put a chair facing Anand, and Yahiya sat on it.

"But, worry not my friend," the man continued. "I am a

great believer of the men who stand for their motherland. You are just like me, haha!" and he continued puffing out clouds of cigar smoke like a dragon.

Anand got confused at this point. Maybe he was trying to deceive him by being nice, maybe it was some kind of international pressure he was acting under, or maybe he was a manipulative psychopath. To test his theory, Wg. Cdr Anand spoke up.

"Nice to meet you too, Chief Yahiya,"

"Ah! The man speaks after all!"

"I think I need a coffee," said Anand.

Yahiya got up from his seat at an instance, took out his service revolver, and directed a shot just past Anand's ear.

It was a surprise to Anand. He was shocked and wasn't sure if he was shot or not. Though he tick-marked one thing. That Air Chief Firoz Yahiya was a manipulative, egoistic psychopath. Trying to dominate him in a conversation would have been an equivalent of a suicide attempt considering Anand's position as a captive. He switched to his quiet mode again to figure out how the crazy man would act.

"You are brave, officer. Indians properly feed their 'protectors' after all! I have seen many wet their pants when I graze their ears with my bullets. You are one of the few who stood the 'lead' test...haha!"

Silence prevailed in the room for the next few seconds. Anand's ears suddenly grew wary of a noise coming close by. The blood-curdling sounds of a man in distress penetrated the walls of the room Anand and Yahiya were in. "Aaaaaa...." a scream and man in the next room screamed with all his might. Yahiya took off Anand's blindfold and smirked, and Anand adjusted his eyes to the poorly lit room. The shrieks of the man were disturbing Anand from the inside. He wanted to help but couldn't. It was as if Firoz Yahiya read his 'Protective' instincts. Though, Anand showed no signs of internal disturbance on the face.

"They are pulling off his nails and teeth with pliers. Poor man! Was probably selling Paki Air Force intel to an ungodly enemy country…In a few hours, we will feed him to our week-hungry hounds," Yahiya said as he fiddled with his lighter. "So, what were you doing in unauthorized airspace?" he asked with a straight face.

"The information and mission intel you carry into the enemy territory is all that stands between you being declared an intruder and prisoner, or being free with minimal damage," Col. Brook lectured the group on political outcomes of the war. "If you find yourself surrounded in the hostile territory, destroy the mission-specific documents, clues, and devices before trying to escape," he said. "It is better to get caught and have the enemy government find nothing on you than them convicting you of intrusion, invasion, etc.

"Let me make this game simple for you, officer. I will ask a question only one time. If you cannot answer, you face the consequences…Understood?"

"I crashed…" Anand finally replied.

"How? How did you crash?" Yahiya lit another cigar.

"I don't know. Probably a bird strike!"

"Hmm…A bird strike! I see…What kind of plane do you fly, officer?" Firoz Yahiya asked as he places his face close to Anand's and stared directly into his eyes. Yahiya's eyes were burning in rage, Anand could tell.

"I don't remember!" Anand couldn't think of a better excuse.

"Haha! Good one," said Yahiya as he made two loud claps. The guards brought him a case of steel and a small wooden tool to keep it on.

Anand knew what it was. He clenched his teeth and hands together to free himself up. But the rope was just too tight.

"You don't fly jet planes, armed with bombs and missiles, officer."

"...I don't remember," Anand was adamant.

"Your enemy will torture you to death if you are of no use to them. If you are of some use, they will hurt you until you speak," Brook addressed the pilots. "Your job as a hostage during an interrogation is to deceive them into thinking that you are invaluable. Someone that they can leverage and negotiate against!" "Will it save us, sir?" a young ace pilot asked. "No. It will buy you some time, though!"

Anand remembered swallowing the mission maps and documents. Others were probably destroyed in the crash.

"Okay. I believe you. The crash hurt your head. You don't remember things. Fair enough. Here, you see. This is a special 'toolbox.' It helps people 'remember,'" said Yahiya in a tone brimming with darkness.

Firoz Yahiya opened the metal case. There laid many kinds of surgical equipment, plumbing equipment, and even butchering equipment. Yahiya took out a small yet sharp and deadly looking surgery knife. The knife's steel shimmered in his hands and

Yahiya said, "You know what we call this? We call this *Inaayat*. It means blessings. "For those who spill our blood and do not follow the path of truth."

"You are going to kill me because my plane crashed because of a bird?" Anand asked him in a rhetorical tone. The 'cool' card was his only chance to escape the fate of merciless torture. "Is this how your country treats its accidental guests?" All Anand was doing was to take slight control of the situation verbally. He knew that Firoz Yahiya was well aware of the dogfight that took place hours ago within the Pakistani LoC.

"I am sure you are a smart man. Being funny is a great way to relieve stress. My wife does that when she messes up. Glad I do not have to use these tools on her," and Yahiya made a small incision with the blade on Anand's right calf. He flinched in pain and clenched his hands as hard as he could.

Firoz Yahiya established that he was 'in charge' in this room and that Wg. Cdr. Anand was at his mercy.

For a moment, Anand could barely breathe. Yahiya immediately called a guard with first aid. "Looks like you are not made for the pain, dear. Let us get started with your mission details," Yahiya said as he wiped the bloodstain on the blade with a small cloth and kept it back, "I have bigger and better 'tool,' remember that…"

Anand was now sure that the Pakistani Govt. wasn't operating under any international pressure. "It was a regular patrol. Bird strike got me down. I have told you before," Anand said. "What made you chase and shoot that bird called F-16?" Yahiya asked with a dead stare at Anand's face.

"He intruded the no-fly zone. He engaged me. I engaged

him back. Nothing personal here," said Anand.

"Hmm...You are a good pilot then. So, you were not in any mission like reconnaissance?" Firoz Yahiya's words were radiating more and more anger. "No. I respect the international laws and policies," Anand said.

Yahiya now took out a big wire cutter from the metal case. He looked behind Anand's shoulder, towards the door. All Anand heard was the heavy metal door shutting behind him.

"International laws! I love the term. You have been acting real smart since you got here. You are brave, I give you that. But often, the brave are fools willing to die." Anand kept looking in the man's eye as he spoke.

"You mean there are no brave, but either fools or cowards?" Anand tried to mock the old man's philosophy. Yahiya smirked, his signature evil stretch of the right dimple and cheek said it all. "You, my friend, will learn a lot about being a coward and a fool in about a second. Now tell me, who instructed you to shoot down a Pakistani jet? Hint, the wrong answer will cost you your index finger!"

"Why don't you check my aircraft's wreckage?" Anand tried to dodge the man's psychopathic behaviour. "Wrong answer. Now you lose a finger, son," the evil man said as he lifted Anand's right hand to sort out the index finger. Anand could do nothing but shut his eyes, honestly, praying he could die a painless death.

The door suddenly opened up before Anand could lose his finger placed on the merciless blades of the cold steel.

"Sir, there is a call from the Defense Minister. Indian Ambassador is on the line," Captain Waseem told Firoz.

Firoz Yahiya's sinister act was halted, as if by the mercy of the Almighty. Anand had another day to live and think.

45

Negotiate a Win

"A good hunter is the one who can kill the beast. A better hunter is the one who can negotiate with his savagery."

"This is a big one, Joseph. We'll need your input on how to arrest the minds behind this dare," the Home Minister said over the call.

"I'll need full cooperation, no bureaucracy, no questions, and intelligence resources," Clinton Joseph was all clear with his demands.

"You've got it. Proceed as you see fit. I'll do the needful, but I need the results ASAP," Home Minister sounded as if the crisis of the pressure will eat him up.

"Sure, sir," Clinton said as the brief call ended.

He unlocked the cell phone's keypad again and dialled a number, "Hey, Leena! Get your cyber-team together. I need you to trace every suspicious communication between Pakistan and Kashmir for the last 3 months. Keep the records intact, I will visit you once it is done." "Got it, sir," Leena, a young cyber-security expert from IIT-Delhi, said to Clinton. Having worked with him on cases of national interest in the past, she was well aware of the gravity that Clinton Joseph held within himself. She knew he was the kind of man who would never ask for anything, but if he does, he would never take 'no' for an answer. "Change of plan Leena, I won't be able to come to Mumbai. As soon as you get the records, encrypt them and fly to Kashmir. We will take it from here," Joseph said. "Will do, sir," Leena affirmed.

Within the next few hours, Joseph found himself in a covert detainment facility for 'highly' contained prisoners somewhere near Jammu.

Joseph walked into the premises as if he owned it. Thick forest surrounded the 4-acre campus making it impossible for ordinary satellites to spot. There was a high-wall topped with barbed wires, about 8-feet tall, surrounding the campus. From the outside, the buildings appeared to be small and old, not worthy of giving any special attention. The locals knew the place to be an 'abandoned' government project. When Joseph walked in, he was escorted to the main building so that he could meet the Commander-in-charge of the place. From the inside, the place was so strongly built it could stand nuclear attacks.

"Hi, Commander Dutta," Joseph had a smile which he kept reserved for only old friends and acquaintances.

"You haven't changed a bit, Clinton," Commander of the BSF Battalion in-charge of the facility, Maj. Anil Dutta greeted him with full honour. "Dolly 3 had not seen her old friend for long. I know what landed you here, let us go to my office."

Dutta escorted the man with 2 special protection guards to his office. Dolly 3, for 'better reasons,' was the code name of this secret facility where the most lethal, dark, aggressive, and passionate criminals of national interest were locked-up, forever!

Clinton sat in front of Dutta on a well-cushioned chair with a giant Pinewood desk separating the duo. "2 Coffees, 1 black and strong," Maj. Dutta ordered over the intercom. Clinton Joseph's smile was now gone. He seemed to be lost somewhere. He was still struggling to process what he had witnessed today. Dutta, being an old friend, understood his nature well, at least enough to gauge his thought process.

"How bad was it?" Dutta asked him with no slightest hint of hesitation. He had been a good friend to Joseph for years now.

"Bad. Something I wish I could unsee," Clinton said as he fiddled with a paperweight on Dutta's wooden desk.

"Been there, done that lad! I know the feeling. What did they use?" Maj. Dutta asked him.

"RDX."

"So how do you want to start?"

"I need to talk to some 'inmates' here. I am sure I'll be able to pull-off some valuable intel. I have a cyber-expert coming to Jammu sometime soon."

"Hmm...Let me know if I can be of help in any way," Dutta offered him all the help he could in his authority.

"Thanks! I appreciate it. Please send someone with me, I'd like to talk to Al-Khaled first."

Dutta held his neck high and after a brief pause said, "Done!" Both the men shook hands and Clinton prepared to leave. "Where is he?" he asked as he shoved the chair under the desk. "Protocol 7. Two storeys below the ground. I'll call in Capt. Patnaik. He will assist you further," Dutta said. Clinton just nodded his head in a way appreciative of what Dutta did.

As he approached the door, Ram Bawa knocked on the office door. "Sir, coffee," he said, taking a peek from outside the door. Ram Bawa was a locally hired staff assistant who undertook all the odd jobs. He was hired as a temporary replacement of the Govt. Peon 3 months back when the ex-employee went to his hometown never to return. Clinton Joseph's detective eye turned to Dutta. "Where is his uniform?" Clinton asked Dutta. "Oh! He is a temporary staff until the new appointment arrives. The previous one was too scared to work here, I guess. He never returned to work," Dutta said.

"Let us postpone the coffee for some other time, huh Major?" Clinton asked as he rushed out to meet Capt. Patnaik.

Dutta sat on his chair, "I am here if you need anything," he said.

Capt. Patnaik was a smart built man, a courageous and sharp person who had been working for the Indian Government for a decade now. Clinton was glad to meet him. It was as if Clinton Joseph found solace in the company of logical and no-nonsense people. Those who preferred to see the world from an emotional perspective often bored him. Emotions once held a place in Clinton's heart. Now it was history.

"Hello, sir! Capt. Patnaik. It is a pleasure," the man greeted Clinton with a hard to miss enthusiasm. "Likewise, Capt." Joseph greeted him with his classical handshake and subtle smile. "Maj. Dutta has appointed me as your attaché to assist you in your investigation. Where would you like to get started, sir?" Patnaik, with his hands folded back, asked Joseph. Joseph gave the man a mysterious smile and said, "Your most cautious protocol, Al-Khaled," as lit up a cigarette in the open compound. "At once, sir. Please follow me," Capt. told Joseph. And the duo fled inside another building of the campus and found themselves in a lift bound downwards in an instance.

"How long has Khaled been in here?" Joseph asked Patnaik just to keep the silence in the lift at bay. He did this not because of himself, but to ease the young Captain's mind around him. "4-years now, sir." Joseph suddenly remembers something and takes out his cell phone. He was hoping for an update from Leena. Without glancing at the investigator's cell phone, Patnaik said," Ah, cell phones or any other electronic device won't work down here. This place is secured with radio jammers, sir." Joseph raised his brow and affirmed the man's statement.

For 90-seconds, the lift crackled its way down the shaft to reach an underground facility. As the doors slid-open, Joseph scanned the surroundings for he had never been at this level of Dolly 3. Patnaik stepped out and showed Clinton Joseph the way forward. Armed personnel heavily guarded this level. There were individual cells that could be identified with metallic doors with a pocket-sized glass pane on them. "So, the enemy of the states are locked up behind them, I see," Joseph made a casual remark. "Not the enemies of the state, sir, enemies of humanity. These men, for the lack of better words, have no sanity or morality when it comes to human blood," Patnaik erased any scope of misconception from Joseph's mind.

The duo walked a few yards forward into the corridor and the armed personnel saluted them as they advanced towards the cell of their interest.

"Number 23. There it is sir," Patnaik pointed Joseph's gaze towards a cell separated from others.

"Is it to be done inside the cell?" Joseph raised his doubt of interrogating within the 'risky' proximity of the dreaded man who once beheaded 3 prisoners with broken glass shrapnel.

"No, sir. We shall move him to the interrogation cell," Patnaik reassured Joseph.

"Terrific!"

Two other armed personnel directed Joseph towards a larger cell with blind glass on one wall. He took his position on the chair opposite to the one where Al-Khaled was to assume his place during the interrogation. Joseph sat down, folded his legs as if sitting on a rocking chair on the weekend, and kept his small memo pad handy. Then began the wait for the arrival of the name, which Joseph had a strong doubt on.

The wristwatch on Joseph's left hand would have clocked less than 5 minutes when the large metal door opened up. There stood the butcher of hundreds of men. His eyes showed no sign of humanity, his hair long and untidy. Al-Khaled's stature resembled those of the barbarians. His limbs were tied down with metal wires and 3 personnel armed with assault rifles led him into the room. The protocol was clear when it came to transporting the 'Inmate 23.' Shoot at sight if he tries to overpower or escape the guards. Khaled slowly walked in and was immediately made to sit on the chair while the 3 guards took their positions in the respective corners of the room.

Al-Khaled was known to send chills down the spines of

others by just staring at them. He never blinked. He was rarely seen sleeping by the security team members. He rarely spoke. And he rarely let any window of opportunity to escape pass-by. For moments, everyone in the room was silent. Joseph kept staring him in the eyes, and Khaled did the same. Interrogation is not just questions and answers, followed by the use of force. It is more of mental warfare, and Clinton Joseph was the medallion in it. He knew, first one to back-off from the 'staring game' would lose, the first one to speak would lose, and the first one to display aggression would lose. Clinton began smiling at the prisoner, and the prisoner mirrored his action. Detective Joseph became more comfortable on the seat, suggesting to Khaled that he handles men of his stature every day, and they often lose.

Clinton opened his pack of cigarettes and lit one for himself. His cigarettes were made of high-quality tobacco, the smoke of which was loved by smokers. It was a soothing blend of many herbs, and being in the prison for many years without any 'luxury,' Al-Khaled's defences were let down by the tempting smoke as it covered the room. Clinton Joseph played his trick well. He knew that the dreaded man in front of him would play nice if offered a cigarette. With no warning, Clinton threw the pack of smoke to one of the guards and asked him to light a cigarette for Khaled.

The dialogue was about to begin.

Nuclear India Vs Pakistan

Experts assess that India is consciously pursuing more flexible options such as having the capability to do hard counterforce targeting. India is likely interested in having some ability to pre-emptively target Pakistan's long-range, strategic nuclear missiles.

This shift in India's declared nuclear strategy of minimum credible deterrence may have been prompted by Pakistan's development of tactical nuclear warheads and missiles. Pakistan has threatened to use these against India's conventional forces if India's forces enter into Pakistan and cross certain redlines. While the whole idea of battlefield nuclear weapons – such as Pakistan is developing – has many complications, India would probably want to have a range of options available to it to respond to any Pakistani use of nuclear weapons on India's conventional forces. India's public nuclear posture/policy calls for massive retaliation against any such nuclear weapon use. This goes hand-in-hand with India's declared policy of 'no first use' (NFU) of nuclear weapons.

But how credible is the idea of a massive counter-value strike against Pakistani cities – leading to the death of millions of innocent civilians – in response to nuclear use on Indian forces operating on Pakistani soil? If India chooses to respond proportionately to Pakistan's use of nuclear weapons, then Pakistan could escalate up the nuclear ladder by targeting high-value Indian cities/ population centers. This is in a way giving the initiative back to Pakistan.

This being the case, India's policymakers/strategic planners are attracted to the idea of having the option of a hard-counterforce strike against Pakistan's land-based strategic nuclear assets. This counterforce strike has fewer credibility issues than a counter value targeting strategy.

Once counterforce strike becomes India's overt or covert nuclear posture, it raises the stakes for Pakistan. It has less incentive to use Theatre Nuclear Weapons (TNWs) and more incentive to go for a full-scale nuclear attack on key Indian assets.

If Pakistan feels compelled to unleash its entire nuclear arsenal before India attempts to disarm them, India will also feel compelled to go for a pre-emptive counterforce strike. But given India's official NFU stance, a pre-emptive strike would violate India's declared nuclear policy. Interestingly, India appears to be subtly shifting the meaning of its NFU policy by saying that pre-emptive nuclear use is okay upon warning of imminent Pakistani nuclear weapon launch.

Having the counterforce option would give India the confidence to wage a conventional war of whatever nature it chooses without having to worry about Pakistan's nuclear blackmail. But there's a risk attached to India's "counterforce temptations."

There is no guarantee that India's pre-emptive strikes against

Pakistan's strategic nuclear assets will be a complete success. Of course, Pakistan will adjust its nuclear posture when it perceives that India's posture has shifted. Both sides might decide that they cannot afford to go second – this will lead to a dangerous "first-strike instability." Since India is unlikely to explicitly deny its interest in counterforce options – and even if it does, Pakistan is unlikely to take such a denial at face value – Pakistan will react to this Indian threat. How might that reaction take shape? It might lead to Pakistan having more nuclear weapons and having them deployed liberally with launch authority perhaps delegated to field commanders in crises.

These "games" have all been played before and at much larger scales than India and Pakistan can ever play. The superpower Cold War rivalry involved tens of thousands of nuclear weapons – at their peak; both sides had more than 50,000 nuclear weapons in total.

Evil over Good

"Sometimes, evil simply wins because it is a split-second faster than the good"

In interrogation rooms, there often comes a moment when one can only hear beating hearts beneath the skin exuding sweat. If one would care to listen closely, one might hear the stained old walls telling stories. Stories of doom, murder, confessions, conspiracies, and innocence. Interrogation rooms have an air of mystery and fright. The environment is often stale and screams of the primal human instincts that drive men to murder their kind with utmost brutality. Joseph had been into such rooms many times. Though, this one was way darker for his taste. The only thing that eased him was the smoke of glowing slow-killers. Khaled sat there placing the smoke over his lips with his cuffed hands, watching Joseph in between.

Al-Khaled murmurs something in his native tongue, trying to pay homage to his almighty.

Joseph: *How do you do that? How do others with you do it?*

Khaled seemed perplexed for a few seconds; "Do what?" he

said and took another puff from a quarter-burnt cigarette.

Joseph: *That. Kill people and dare to summon God. Does your almighty fancy blood, does he like screams of the men when they are being beheaded? Does he like it when people get bombed?*

Khaled smirked. He raised his head higher, forced a fake smile, and said," Almighty? What do you know of him? What do you know about God? You are a man on Govt. Payroll….". Joseph let Khaled continue. "You are a man who is taken care of, by the family, by the public, by the country, and by your 'GOD'" said Khaled as his voice shivered with suppressed rage. Clinton Joseph could sense it very well and positioned himself like the keenest listener in the world.

Khaled: *'Innocent' people have one annoying quality. They turn their eyes in the face of darkness, blame others who could never overcome the circumstances, and they reason."*

Joseph: *They reason?*

Khaled ground his teeth in frustration as if a teacher would do when fed up with silly questions by the young students. "Citizens, civilized people, or whatever you may label them, they develop a veil of 'blindness' by what you call education. They think blasphemy is right, killing is wrong, they become weak and unable to protect what is important. All their lives, they hide behind 'reasons' and 'justifications' of what is right and wrong…" said the man in cuffs as he took a deep breath. The underground room was a little hot and humid and all the three people there were sweating without flinching.

Joseph couldn't fathom the right starting point to talk sense to the man. Al-Khaled was too hardened and brainwashed to accept any idea of rationality. Though, Joseph played it fair in the beginning.

Joseph: *Blindness? Justifications? Do you think anyone who does not agree with extremist ideology deserves death?*

Khaled: *I am nobody to decide who lives or dies. I follow the commandments of my God. My purpose is to spread this message and protect the interests of my 'Almighty' against those who are cleverly destroying them.*

Joseph: *So, you are not a terrorist but a mercenary?* Khaled just threw a dead stare into the man's eyes for a reply. "Leave it," said Joseph, "We can talk like this all night and reach nowhere," and he signalled the guard to bring him the pack of smokes.

"So... how is your clan, how are your brothers in the field doing?" asked Joseph with a smile, his head held high in confidence. Khaled kept silent, occasionally stealing his gaze away from the detective.

"The silence game, huh! You were mumbling a lot of philosophy a few moments ago. Now you don't want to talk. I suggest let's talk. Let us save ourselves precious time," and Joseph leans closer to the man to whisper something," I have heard they don't give you alcohol in here. And you haven't met your girlfriend in a while, right?"

As Joseph leans back, Khaled raises his gaze to look back into the detective's eyes. A burst of wild laughter then ensued. The old-stained room walls with their sad stories had heard such giggles, perhaps, after decades.

It was Al-Khaled who was laughing. The guard shifted his eyes towards Joseph, and Joseph raised his eyebrows, though he wasn't surprised. He kept smoking and watched Khaled's cigarette end.

"Why bother with the laughter?" Joseph asked with a face of a veteran investigator. "You guys are unbelievable," said Khaled as he gradually halted his laugh. "You are trying to bribe me with booze and girls?" and he went into another fit of uncontrolled laughing. When the laughter wore off after a few odd seconds, he said, "Don't you think I knew about what jails are like? You are going to bribe me so I betray the trust of my God and my brethren on the mission?" and Khaled's voice again radiated hidden aggression in his voice.

Khaled: *You think I am like a corrupt clerk like the ones in your government who'd sell out everything for some cheap booze and girls? Who recruited you, man?*

Joseph chose not to answer this and kept looking at him as if he wanted him to continue speaking.

Khaled: *You wear a white-collar shirt with a nice watch, Mr. Clinton. You like to smoke the best cigarettes and attend parties with big-shots. You pretend to be doing a service to the nation. You live far from the truth, far from reality…*

Joseph did nothing but kept staring at him as if he was being offended by the man. Though, inside his head, he just wanted Khaled to speak out any trash he would. He wanted the dreaded killer and a national enemy to let his defences down as he spoke.

Joseph: *You don't like my clothes or cigarettes?* And he laughed as if mocking the man as he spoke. *Hey, officer, do you like my clothes?* Joseph went on mocking the man's conviction. The prison guard stood there, without laughing or smiling, placing his pointer-finger over the trigger lightly enough to noose the muzzle of his assault rifle.

At this point, Khaled was offended. His face told so.

Khaled: *Your kind does not seem to get it. Your people pretend to form an army, pretend to protect the citizens, and pretend to protect the order of the society. The truth is… The truth is, we are the ones who have to cleanse the dirt!*

Joseph looked directly into the man's eyes as if trying to find traces of humanity behind them. He failed and asked, "Cleanse who?"

Khaled: *Those who hate the strong, those who destroy our culture. The people from the west and east have zeroed in on us for long. They are the invaders, afraid of our God. For long, they have prostituted us to the west, destroyed our culture, and polluted our women. But pests like you and your government have forgotten one thing. That we are the warriors, the Jihadis. You have forgotten that we are not shy of bloodshed. We have been ruling the world since Genghis Khan. We will rule the world tomorrow…*

Khaled's words came to rest as he gloated and glanced at Joseph in a taunting manner. Joseph kept staring at him with the same old calm demeanour. He wasn't allowed to touch the highly secured prisoner of national interest. Though, in the field, he wouldn't have spared the gloating man alive. So far, Clinton Joseph was successful in getting the man to open his mouth, something which was thought to be impossible by Maj. Dutta.

Joseph: *Correct me if I am wrong here, you moron. You say that innocent children and women have destroyed your culture and struck your 'God' powerless?* Joseph raised his right brow and slowly leaned forward. *Are you justifying all the mess you have created, all the people you have murdered with a simpleton's logic?*

And the detective's words were ensued by another short-lived laugh from the man of monstrous predisposition.

Khaled: *This. I wanted to hear this for long. So badly. I like it when people like you get angry. You get angry when you get hurt. I do not 'kill' people. My men don't 'murder' innocent men, women, and children. We 'Sacrifice' them for Allah, we sacrifice them to hurt your system and cleanse it of pollution.* Khaled smiled as he talked. His smile was the most disgusting one Joseph had ever seen.

It was tough for the detective, a man is known for his patience and deep-thought traits, to grasp the beliefs the man in front of him held of the world. Dark, hateful, and thirsty for blood. How do we make a person into such a thing, he wondered? Though, he kept his fists clenched and pushed the discourse further.

Joseph: Sacrifice?? You call that sacrifice, huh? Interesting how evil works! And Joseph's face bought up one of those frustrations oozing failed smile that once manifested when his love parted away. *You haven't met the right kind of 'God' I guess. You haven't been served justice, my friend. You will be rewarded fairly for all your 'sacrifices.' Not in heaven, but here on Earth.*

Khaled looked at him as if observing a man of fading intelligence. Yet Joseph's confidence and the gleam in his eyes chiselled a small mark of terror in his heart.

Joseph: Deep down you know your fate, man. Your masters are sitting far behind the LoC, probably sipping the finest champagne and thinking about your 'replacement.' You are an expendable resource, moron! Joseph stood up, turned his back towards Khaled, and started walking around the room.

"You think you won their hearts? Haha, you were always a fool to them. They manipulated you, used you, made you do inhumane things to the innocent so that their hands remain clean. You are nothing but a butcher on hire who thinks he is doing some holy job. In reality, you are just a blind delusional who derives joy from sadism. You are an enemy to humanity, a rabid dog who must be put down at the first sight…" Joseph went on. His words came out with a dual purpose. He wanted to steam out his wisdom to teach the delusional terrorist, and the second purpose was to escalate the man's temperament so that he throws out some valuable information.

"In my long career, I have had the honour to put down a few rabid dogs like you. I cannot describe the feeling of elation I get when I see your brethren cold and dead in government mortuaries…haha," and Joseph lit up another cigarette.

Al-Khaled: *I got the same rush…My men put down 40 something dogs of yours with an IED (Improvised Explosive Device) …Hahaha.* Khaled's laughing fit hit him again. Joseph stopped and pondered.

Joseph: *So, they were your men? Who else was involved in your job? Answer me if you are a man not born of a brothel!*

Khaled: *Losing dignity there are we, officer? Such words don't suit your personality. It doesn't matter to you if I am born of a brothel or not. Haha…I have been through much smarter interrogators like you. Let me spare both of us some time.*

Joseph stood there all alert so as not to miss any word of importance he spoke. A date, a number, a name, anything! The protection officer in the room also switched his stance to listen better.

Joseph: *Go on.*

Al-Khaled: *Yes. I was the one behind the recent blast, I designed the full 'Solution.' I operated the whole game while your government stood helpless. I divided your men into small pieces of meat to offer to my*

Allah. A few KGs of RDX, a Car, and two men were all I needed. I gave them the instructions right till the last moment. I heard the blast trigger over the phone. I could only imagine the scene when your men screamed, dead, wounded, scared...That was my mission right there. I wanted to see them scared. When I see the terror in the eyes of the 'Kafirs, 'I move one step closer to salvation. I will do it again; I will sacrifice more people. My men will wage a war against every 'Kafir' born on this land. And we are not afraid. Not afraid to die, not afraid to go to hell, not afraid of the pain of judgment. We will strike you back at every opportunity. We will cut out the throats of your people, pollute your women, take-away your children, and plant our flags everywhere.

Khaled's breathing went heavy, almost to the point where his brain nerves would burst with rage. Joseph kept listening to him clenching his jaws.

Khaled: *And your God is with us today.* Joseph got a little puzzled. *Thanks to your inferior bloodline, you cowards. Your men can be bought with money so easily.*

The terrorist stopped abruptly. "How is that? How did our 'God' help you, Khaled?" asked Joseph.

Khaled looked up, closed his eyes, and appeared to be reciting to his almighty. His head lowered back parallel to the floor. He smiled. "Your Ram was never on your side...Hahaha... Hahaha," and he clipped away his locket, placed it inside his mouth, and said, "Khuda-Hafiz, Afsaraan. Allah-Hu-Akbar," and he swallowed whatever was there inside the locket

Before the other officer could understand anything, Joseph moved swiftly towards the terrorist to open up his jaw forcefully. Too late though, he was already dead.

Impatience to death or defeat

"Impatience is a classical sign of hot blood. It is the one that kills and gets killed."

The whirring of the jet engine died out and the after-burners started to cool. Just beneath the canopy was a graffiti that read 'Hellraiser.' The canopy lifted and *Young Thunder* climbed down the metal ladder that was just placed by an Airman. He was in a hurry, more than usual. The airman saluted him but he did not take notice of him. He undid his flying helmet, gave his pressurized jacket to the order, and frantically walked towards the hanger.

In the green Mechanic suit patched with the Indian flag stood Air Force Chief Technician, Siddhartha Awasthi. His hands were folded back and his expression lacked a smile, which was usually there. The pilot stood in front of him. Squadron Leader Mrityunjai Mandal, or as Wing Commander Anand titled him, *Young Thunder* was one of the most precious pilots in the force. He trained under Anand and was the youngest ace pilot of the squadron. For once, Mrityunjai grinned and looked away.

"Look. You were on the mission. You know the protocol. There was nothing we could have done to inform you," Mr. Awasthi explained. Mandal soaked in the explanation, made an ape-like face to conceal his disappointment, then relaxed. "Kaka, you know what *Anna* means to me. He is not just my senior. He is my Godfather," said Mandal. Siddhartha nodded to show empathy, and the duo began moving towards the hangar.

"So, how bad is it? When is he coming back?" Mandal asked. Awasthi paused for a while and then said, "He has been captured, but we-..." before he could resume another word, Mandal burst out- "*Anna* is in captivity? By Pakistan? You are telling this to me now, Siddhartha?"

"Protocol-"

Mandal almost said something and then closed his eyes, his head up. "What now, what are we doing?"

"The delegation is in the talks. We are yet to hear any statement from them or Anand," Awasthi said.

Awasthi motioned over to a staff member and he immediately bought over a cup of coffee. Mandal took no notice and sat upon a bean bag. "I'll shower first," he said. "Good! Good idea," Awasthi acknowledged. "Then bring *Anna* back. Then I'll have that goddam coffee," Mandal said as he rose again from the bean bag.

"See. This is exactly why Anand named you *Young Thunder*. Behind that cool pet-title is a reason. You are hot-headed like actual thunder, and you are volatile. Anand and I used to discuss your temper. If he were here, he would've...," Awasthi continued but was interjected by Mandal, "He would have if he were here. He is not. That is what." The young pilot headed towards the flying officer's mess.

Siddhartha had been one of the most sought-after technical experts of the Dassault manufactured Mirage 2000-C aircraft. From avionics to armament, he could repair the thing in the dark with just a screwdriver, as the squadron would often joke. Though, it was not his technical skills that had won him a special place in the 79th Bomber Squadron officers' hearts. He could resolve, build relationships, and guide even the officers who functioned above him. They would often reciprocate the same respect because of his attitude and ethics. Siddhartha Awasthi had a notion that Mandal will initiate something, and might land up in trouble because of his temper. This had happened on several occasions. This was happening now when he got the news of the ongoing in the Air Marshal's office.

One of Siddartha's colleagues called him up. "What? Damn. I knew it. Okay, keep me updated," Awasthi said as he hung up the phone.

It was a highly decorated office and every object was placed with precision. There were medals on the wall, rare paintings, a fine cabinet of imported malts, and scale models of numerous aircraft. Air Marshal Dhanoba was a highly decorated leader of the Indian Air Force's deadliest bomber squadron. Dhanoba sat in his enormous leather chair, stroking his beard.

Three Squadron Leaders, Mrityunjai Mandal, Amandeep Singh, and Param Pasrisha stood at attention in front of him. "At ease, gentlemen," Dhanoba said in the voice of an old lion king.

"A strike? A covert strike to rescue Anand? Gentlemen, I understand your emotions. But the government has already intervened. It is not just the prestige of the Air Force at stake, but a matter of international relations now. We cannot take autonomous actions," he said.

"Sir, may I?" Mandal asked.

"Yes, officer."

"Wg. Cdr. Anand is one of us. I am sure he'd be expecting an exfil mission. I say we plan a deep strike overnight, bomb the surroundings, extract our officer in a chopper, and fly away. Plausible deniability," Mandal said in a single breath.

"Good plan, Officer! But I am sure that we are way past the 'Plausible Deniability' escape card. Anand is the Indian Government's responsibility now. IAF will only work as per the orders," Dhanoba said. "No more funny ideas. I am sure we will bring him back as he went. Any questions?"

"But sir..." Mandal intervened.

"Any more questions?" Dhanoba roared.

"No sir," the officers said in a unison.

As Mandal walked out of the Marshal's office, Awasthi patted his back. "He is the *Cheetah* son. You don't know about Anand's capability. He is dangerous, not vulnerable."

Join the Force

"Obviously, a halo of general merit is extended to influence the rating for the special ability, or vice versa."

American Psychologist - Edward Thorndike

The 'halo effect' was another fascinating concept that had something to do with the profession of the armed forces. It had to do with the subtle difficulties that arise in situations where people have to evaluate other people. Danny Kahneman designed the questions for the interviewers recruiting for the Israel Defence Forces such that he could bypass this halo effect.

Thorndike went on to say that he had "become convinced that even a very capable foreman, employer, teacher, or department head is unable to view an individual as a compound of separate qualities and to assign a magnitude to each of these in the independence of the others."

So, if interviewers judged someone as 'smart' and 'dashing' in terms of personality, they might then also go ahead and give a positive opinion about his physique. Assessment of one aspect of a person tended to influence the assessment of another, unrelated aspect.

Anand thought that maybe this could cloud people's judgment of political leaders as well. If people 'liked' a politician for some reason, then they would tend to give that politician a 'pass' on other matters even though the politician may have performed poorly objectively on several parameters. This is where ideology came into play and perhaps how demagogues did well – they knew how to take advantage of people's biases.

As an Air Force pilot, Anand found Danny Kahneman's experience with the Israeli Air Force (IAF) instructive. Danny had noticed that IAF instructors believed that the 'students' reacted better to criticism than to praise. The instructors believed that criticism was more useful than praise.

Michael Lewis has written in The Undoing Project:

The instructors 'explained to Danny that he only needed to see what happened after they praised a pilot for having performed especially well, or criticised him for performing especially badly. The pilot who was praised always performed worse the next time out, and the pilot who was criticised always performed better. Danny watched for a bit and then explained to them what was going on: The pilot who was praised because he had flown exceptionally well, like the pilot who was chastised after he had flown exceptionally badly, simply were regressing to the mean. They'd have tended to perform better (or worse) even if the teacher had said nothing at all. An illusion of the mind tricked teachers – and probably many others – into thinking that their words were less effective when they gave pleasure than when they gave pain. Statistics wasn't just boring numbers; it contained ideas that allowed you to glimpse deep truths about human life.

"Because we tend to reward others when they do well and punish them when they do badly, and because there is regression to the mean," Danny later wrote, "it is part of the human condition that we are statistically punished for rewarding others and rewarded for punishing them."'

There is probably a lesson in this for pilots as well as parents and school teachers.

In making decisions and judgments about events that are uncertain or probabilistic, humans make systematic errors. Humans are prone to biases and humans don't understand randomness. Anand found this fascinating but also alarming. How would decision-makers decide about the use of fighter aircraft in a conflict situation? How would the leadership in India and Pakistan evaluate and interpret the often imperfect signals from the opposite side in a fluid and uncertain situation such as war? Might we not stumble into a nuclear war because of some biases that most people – including leaders – are prone to?

People must at least be aware of the imperfections of our mind. Londoners erroneously thought during the Second World War that German bombs were targeted; they were not. Statisticians showed that random bombing would lead to some parts of a city getting bombed repeatedly.

How good would people be in judging whether a candidate will be elected to political office or whether a 12-year-old boy will grow up to be a scientist?

Good Vs Evil

"Evil is born of the darkness, good is born of the light. The former is always conceived when the latter is absent"

They were closing the coffins one by one. Sealed them with the plastic for the flight. I stood right there, beside the medical officer who was tallying the body count. He had a horrible job and my respect grew for him. Almost no coffin carried a complete body. I don't know what ate my soul away yesterday morning. The fact that those who died, their souls will be feeling pity seeing their loved ones weeping, or the way the family members will live the rest of their lives knowing the 'state' in which their men died valiantly? As the team began loading the coffins into the C-130 Hercules Cargo aircraft, the whirring of the giant propellers made me oblivious to the world. I have seen pain. Closely, but this was different. This incident was a personal attack on my soul, trauma to my spirit. I wondered if I'd need a lifetime to recover or even forget about it. It was raining in the morning. The aircraft soon took off and was bound to Delhi airport. I kept looking at the big flying beast until it vanished in the thick shade of clouds. That moment reminded me of my mother's bedtime stories. She used to tell me how angels take away the most adorable and pious children with them. I used to ask her why an angel would separate a child from his parents. To this, she used *to say- "This world is too good for some souls to exist. Angels decide who goes with them." In her story, I found comfort in the thought that there is someone sentient and omnipotent looking at us from above. That sentient power can deliver justice. It saves children and good people from evil. I was a child back then. "Has little Jane gone with the angels too?" I always asked her back. She used to look like my growing curiosity was not a gift but a thorn growing up her forehead. "Yes, Clinton," she said every single time. Now, when I am old enough to realize the sadness that prevails in this world, I know she did not get bugged over my question. She was bugged because I kept repeating that question to her, swinging my mother's soul back into the traumatic memories of the days, when she lost her youngest child. Repeating the questing while knowing the answer, though, was a way for me to pacify myself. Today, I stand here, helpless. I miss my mother. I miss my little brother. As the plane vanished over the horizon, I can pretend that it was an angel. But, whom would I ask for the reassurance that the martyred men have rightly gone to the heavenly abode? I fail to find anyone capable of giving me a reassuring 'yes' to the most perplexing question I have for them. I cannot find them everywhere. I cannot write more. The thoughts are too confusing and overwhelming. I shall come back at a better time to sort all the important questions of existence and find an answer to them. Till then, I have a job to complete and justice to serve.*

Goodnight Diary!

Lovingly

Clinton Joseph

Joseph closed his old diary and stood near the window with his eyes fixed arbitrarily on the elements of nature the next morning. The thoughts of the attack, the confrontation with

Khaled, and the unsolved puzzle were crippling his mind as the time slept out of his hands like sand. He kept calm and went out for a smoke.

"Khaled had started talking… that was rare. I felt that was my win… just when I gained confidence… He had been a step ahead. Had I been too much in the awe of my success to notice it?"

He blamed himself for the failure of interrogation. But deep down, a part of him had confidence in him. A tiny bit in his heart assured him that he was right, it was not his fault. Psychologically, this is not incorrect too! Taking all the burden of a failure on a single self would mostly result in adverse effects over the mind and will shake the confidence.

As his light steps trod over the fresh green grass bathed in morning dew, the cold, hard face came alive in front of him. There was unwinnable anxiety inside Joseph. What makes a human extraordinary? What are some extraordinary career options? People win Nobel Prizes in Physics and other subjects. Doctors save lives. Scientists gain a measure of insight into the workings of nature that only very few ever acquire.

Whether it's Stephen Hawking or Albert Einstein or Richard Feynman or others like him, it's probably impossible for ordinary humans to make sense of the working of the minds of these geniuses. Hawking is well known only because of his special condition – a man trapped inside an almost useless physical body but whose mind soared across the universe and tried to understand something as mysterious as black holes.

Joseph kept walking while his mind jogged through all these thoughts.

He went on to think about the conversation he had with

Khaled earlier. At a distance, a quail screeched somewhere near the valley. Joseph was entangled between two questions. Why did Khaled mention God failing them? Why did he die? There was something very unsettling about this whole scenario. Joseph drags a lawn chair and almost falls on it, facing the patio ridden with red valley flowers. The garden's peace is snapped by the cell phone ring. Joseph glances at the caller ID and hesitates to pick it up. 'Not in a mood of questions,' he thinks. Khaled committed suicide and Joseph will have to bear the load of investigation. Reluctantly, he swipes the green bar on the screen.

"Clinton? The Minister is busy. I am his PA Gopeshwar," the PA continued over the call while the silence prevailed on the other end. "Clinton, the Minister would like to talk to you regarding yesterday's incident at 'the facility,' and just to give you a heads up, he is not happy," Gopeshwar said. "Why?" Joseph asked in a flat, unmoved tone as he puffed down the cigarette. "Pakistani government is aggressively advertising this incident as torture by our defence forces. They are seeking international support and Amnesty international is likely to take this incident pretty seriously." "But everyone in the picture realizes that the man was a vicious piece of shit! Right? Indian forces have suffered a massive attack recently? Never mind the bureaucrats. I'll answer to the minister," Joseph said in an obviously flat but sharp voice. "Ok," Gopeshwar said. Clinton slipped the cell phone back into the packet. 'Dutta will be roped in this investigation too!' And as his mind was swirling in the storm of confusion, he suddenly remembered the small piece of paper he was carrying all this time. *'34 Strides to the North, 73 strides to the East, our 1,24,000 Prophets stand together to hail the almighty...*" he murmured to himself. Intuition came as a gift to Clinton Joseph. He could not connect everything at this moment. Though, with Khaled ingesting cyanide and this statement recovered by the NIA, Joseph's mind could smell something very shady. 'Something big and destructive is brewing,' he thought.

"Sir," a voice came to him, "Sir, a lady, Leena, is here," Powal said to Clinton. Joseph sighed, a little relieved and delighted as he now had someone reliable, someone from the past that he could count on. Without changing his expressions, he asked Powal Ji to get her seated and prepare tea. Joseph took long strides and in the next few moments, he saw Leena standing in the drawing-room by the big black couch. She was a fairly beautiful lady in her 30s, black frame spectacles covered the top half of her perfectly formed face, her thin lips and a light scar on the cheek made her a quickly recognizable person to Joseph. Both of them exchanged smiles, and Leena was glad to be of help to him. "Please, make yourselves comfortable," he said as he shook her soft hands that were protected by her fine black corporate style suite. 'Long time, sir," she said with a smile that revealed her perfectly structured bright white teeth. Clinton smirked something that allowed Leena to read his state of mind. "By now you might be familiar with the situation, I guess?" he asked. She nodded lightly, "And the Khaled incident. I guess it did not turn out to be how you intended." "You have been through, old Leena style," and he gave a little 'bossy' laugh. However, Leena was a lady of whims and wits. She knew her former boss' thought process very well. And so, the duo functioned efficiently as a team.

"I have a task for you. Alright?" Joseph said without actually waiting for her response as he fiddled with the ring on his left hand. "I have a confidential statement. I need you to work on it," and he handed her the black little pouch. She moved partially forward, bent over the couch to grab the pouch. It was Leena's habit to not ask any question until the speaker did himself. "I need you to solve the chit in there. It is probably a cipher. Usually,

I love solving them, the puzzles," Clinton said as he lit another cigarette from his pack. The flame from the lighter shone in his eyes. He gestured to offer Leena a smoke, and she was glad to accept it. The flight had been long and tiring for her. She lit her cigarette, leaned back, and listened. "It was recovered by the NIA in 2013 by a looney in captivity. The surprising thing is, he also committed suicide by ingesting one of those damned pills," he went on, "Fast forward to yesterday, the same thing happened with Khaled. This is enough of a coincidence for me to consider it seriously. I think something big is cooking," he finished as the long stream of tobacco smoke blew out of his nostrils. "You want me to decipher it?" "Yes," he said.

Powal served tea to both of them and went away as they sat in silence. It was not an awkward silence, though. They both loved to solve problems mentally and compete. Solving puzzles gave them the rush and kept their professional chemistry in sync. "There is your room. Be prepared, this house is going to be your home for the next few days. While you work on the cipher, I'll handle the ministry. They'll need something for an answer," he said while staring at his teacup. "I'll get started right away, boss," she said, adjusting her sparkling spectacles. '34, 75, 1,24,000...Seems like a series? a password? a message?' Leena's brain worked on the cipher as Clinton became busy with his phone.

The Sacrificial Lamb

"If the lamb defies the butcher, it only prolongs its death, not escape it."

The black SUV pulled up by the front walls of the Dolly 3 campus, just a few yards from its main gate. The front doors were flung ajar, and Leena and Clinton stepped out. Leena unplugged the vehicle's key-locked it with a chirping alarm and the duo strode towards the entrance. The concrete grey metal door was unobvious in the woods and in no time, they were within the safe confines of the building as an officer hosted them in. "You must be wondering why I asked you to accompany me here," Clinton said to Leena. Her eyes scanned the heavily guarded building, and she glanced at Clinton without any overt expression to let him continue. "I believe you would have the transcript of my 'talk' with Khaled," to which Leena nodded in affirmation.

"Something is puzzling about the whole interview. I am just not able to pin it. While you work on the cipher, I gave you, I want you to dig deeper into it," Clinton said as the duo followed the officer towards Dutta's office.

"What does your gut say, sir?" She asked.

"Khaled taking his own life was the second incident of this type. I can smell the dead fish, but I don't know where it is!" he said as they both glanced at Dutta approaching them just as they reached his office door.

Welcoming as always, Major Dutta greeted them and led them inside the office. The office was mildly cold, yet the heater gave a sense of warmth. "Tea or coffee, gentlemen?" Dutta asked. "I am well, thanks," Joseph replied as he stroked his chin with his right index digit and thumb. "I can do with a coffee, thanks," Leena said as she opened up her laptop screen. "Sure," Dutta said as he pinged the call-bell kept on his table. Ram Bawa, the caretaker, entered the office with due permission. "Two coffees, please," Dutta ordered him. Bawa bowed as he retreated his steps back, and for no reason, Clinton turned to take notice of him. He could not notice his face. All he had was a blemished memory of a caretaker who was now serving the officers because of staff shortage.

"I was expecting you here, Clinton," Dutta broke the ice. "I suppose you are running with the team," he said as he made a gesture towards Leena that demanded her full introduction. "This is Leena. RAW. Came from Mumbai to help us get out of the mess. Old colleague," Clinton said as he fiddled with a glass paperweight on the table. "Very well. You have our full cooperation. Feel free to proceed as you see fit," Dutta allowed them to carry on the investigation. "Okay. How'd you like to begin, Leena?" Clinton asked. "Let us talk to the inmates closest to Khaled. Perhaps, Major Dutta can provide us a list for the same," she said. "It won't be a list. There are a few countable names close to Khaled in the cells. That might help you!" "Sure," she nodded.

The trio trickled down two floors beneath the ground level in an elevator. "You'll kill us all inside," Dutta joked as Clinton lit another cigarette inside the elevator. Leena paid no attention to small talk. She was busy with herself, in her mind, the safest place she had known since her childhood. Leena was a troubled kid. She used to get into terrible fights with her college mates. One time, she scratched a girl's face over name-calling. She often lost it when her family's name got involved. And it was tough for her during those years. Leena's mother eloped with an unknown man. Her father shot himself when she was fourteen years old. Drugs, boyfriends, reckless attitude, and self-sabotaging behaviour defined this beyond beautiful and ingenious lady. The brief elevator ride rekindled the bitter past of glory. For some unknown reason, Leena found herself trapped in those thoughts. The lift thudded to the floor, stopped with a clung. Dutta leads the duo to a well-lit room that contained two officers. "This is Captain Mahim," Dutta said as the officers saluted him. Clinton took a brief note with his hard-sharp eyes, nodded.

In front of the room was a large one-way screen. To the left wall from the screen, a slab carried a few computer systems, communication equipment, and non-lethal weaponry. "You don't like to use lethal, huh?" Joseph asked in his classical tone of criticism. "Imagine what the lethal will do if even one of them got loose!" Maj. Dutta gave a befitting reply to which Clinton said, "So much for the confidence in your system?" and he raised his forehead briefly. Major Dutta did not seem too glad about his remark and let it pass. Leena was clever enough to sense the invisible tension between the two of them, though, both would have refuted her observation.

"I'd like to visit Khaled's cell. I guess it would be vacant for now?" she asked. Dutta simply nodded in affirmation. He took an electronic key from a small locker and came back, "Many of the prisoners still don't know about Khaled's fate. The incident happened in isolation. There is a rumour that he had either escaped or has been transferred elsewhere." He flipped the key open and signalled the duo to follow him. Capt. Mahim followed by default. As they walked, Dutta asked them to keep the rumour continued for better investigative results. "Mahim will bring the requested prisoner to you in the interrogation room," he said. As the group entered the open hallway, on the collar of which were dark cells sealed-off by metal gates. Each cell-row was guarded by a prison guard. There were a total of 9 guards along the hallway, each standing at a distance of 20 yards from the next guard. Mahim and Dutta halted before a grey metal door. This door was far from all the other cell doors. There was a small screen to the right at the standing eye-level. Dutta gave the key to Mahim, and he showed it to the electronic detector placed a foot to the right from the door onto the wall. The door unclunged after a buzzer. Mahim then used the metal blade of the key to unlock the door manually.

It was dark and dingy. The walls gave off a familiar but unrecognized stench. Though, Leena became unsettled when the light was turned on. For the sake of safety, the powerful light hung high from the ceiling to keep it from the malicious intents. Prisoners were allowed only 2 hours of light in the night. This 'luxury' was not to appease the Human Rights Committee but to keep them from going insane.

Leena placed her fingers softly on the dreaded walls, slowly raised her steps, and began moving along the walls of the cellar. On the walls were poorly drawn caricatures. There were phrases and numbers written in Urdu. It was all random. "How did he draw these?" Clinton asked. "His nails," Mahim said. "Every night, he would begin scratching the walls and other prisoners would complain. But there was no stopping him." Everyone began taking a closer look at the walls as if it was an attraction from a circus. On the right wall from the entrance was a drawing that caught everyone's attention.

Carved in the plastered wall was a sensuous figure of a half-dressed lady. Her curves gave the impression of a living figurine, her eyes seemed to look through the soul. She was decorated with a fair amount of jewellery. On the navel of the image was carved the word *Liba.*

"He sure was a romantic, huh," Clinton jokes to break-off the weirdness surrounding the room. Leena exchanged looks briefly with him while Dutta and Mahim seemed busy studying the walls. "Liba, what could that mean?" Clinton asked unspecifically to the group. "Khaled's wife, girlfriend, lost love, maybe! multiple possibilities," Dutta said as his eyes scanned every inch of the beautiful carving.

"So *Liba* might have been her lover?" Mahim asked inquisitively, hoping for support. "Maybe. This seems something else to me," Leena said.

Dutta and Clinton turned towards her; hands folded. "I believe people who draw their loved ones in a fit of what you'd call craziness rarely give attention to detail. To them, the self-expression holds meaning rather than the sketch itself. Whereas, this drawing is full of passion, rage, and devotion. You said he used his nails," she pointed to Mahim. He nodded yes. "This figurine has more to do with religious devotion than anything else," she said.

A moment of silence prevailed and everyone in the cellar

could almost hear each other's thoughts. "Time to talk to some 'friends' now!" said Clinton with a thunder clap that echoed in the cellar, him stepping out of the containment.

***

It was the famed interrogation room, and that brown squeaking wooden chair caught Joseph's attention. Mahim got another chair arranged beside the one where Clinton Joseph sat last time. "Major Mahim will take the charge now, Gentlemen. He will do the needful," said Dutta as he shook the hands of the investigating duo. "Thanks for the cooperation," Leena said. "Indeed," said Dutta as he turned around and his boots trotted out mechanically towards the elevator corridor.

The duo sat in the chairs and Mahim went out of the room to begin the interviews. Leena unpacks her memo and Clinton sat there gazing absentmindedly towards the door. Leena rolls her eyes towards him. "Do you think Khaled might have had accomplices in here?" Clinton took a deep breath and nodded yes as he said, "It is probable."

Six hours long interviews didn't reveal new facts to the duo. Khaled used to talk to a few prisoners. One of them had revealed about his poetic side, another one about his food habits. The investigators kept trying in vain. However, on Clinton's wit, the duo began investigating Khaled's potential enemies from the cellar.

The idea worked better than anticipation. A prisoner spoke up. This sour-turned friend of Khaled revealed that Khaled 'used to talk a lot about God's revenge plan on those who committed sacrilege. And, about how an army of Prophets is being prepared to run over the enemy.' And The investigators easily trusted the story. Because Khaled 'killed' the aid that supplied drugs to him.

"Who was the aid?" Leena asked eye-to-eye… "it was a staff member," he said. "You say he was killed…?" She asked. "Yes. A few months back. I haven't been able to sleep since. He bought me a good fix every week." "What did he bring you?" she strengthened the gaze. A moment of silence ensued. The man said, "Opium…" "Why did he do that?" Clinton asked again. "He owed me big time. He was almost beaten to death one day by the inmates. I saved him. He owed me," the prisoner said.

The pain inside Anand grew with time. Neither did it let him live, nor did it let him sleep. Anand felt as if the pain would consume his thinking capabilities. And that maybe the win the enemies were expecting. Anand let some of the bright, colorful memories pour back in. and in fact, he started to recall them, which he thought might take his attention off the pain and keep his mind from the negative thoughts.

Anand and Nandini were realists and not given to flights of fancy. Both had jobs to do. Both kept busy with their air force commitments. Their marital life was mostly without discord and in a few years, they were the proud parents of a boy and a girl. Nandini made the difficult decision to leave the air force once she reached her mandatory minimum of 15 years of service.

They planned a vacation up in the north once Nandini was retired from the air force. They went to the little town of Mukteshwar up in the Garhwal Himalayas. You had to pass through the crowded hill station of Nainital and then through the winding roads up the mountains. You skirt Saattal and Bhimtal before you reach Mukteshwar.

It was a relaxed seven-day holiday. They had booked a room

in a small hotel there. Water was scarce at 7000+ feet above sea level though there were several lakes as the word 'tal' signifies.

They emptied their brains of flying rosters and other professional information and relaxed for a few days. They could walk about aimlessly on the steep roads or just sit by the roadside. At night, the stars were countless and incredibly bright – a far cry from what city dwellers experience.

He recalled Randy Pausch's The Last Lecture. Another story of a life and a career cut short in full bloom and at its peak. He recalled the positive attitude Dr. Pausch showed, the sunny demeanour, in his interviews. Maybe it was a façade? An 'act' for the cameras? What did Dr Pausch have to say about his impending death from which there was no escape? Anand didn't remember much and made a mental note to catch up with the video later. He would have watched the video there and then if there was internet in the mountains but unfortunately all that still lay ahead in the future.

"Do you remember Dr. Randy Pausch and his book and video called The Last Lecture?" Anand asked.

"Who? Yes …." Nandini replied. She was overseeing the kids eating. North Indian default food like rotis or chapattis were still a bit of a novelty for the kids. The kids enjoyed naan with butter chicken. Neither Nandini nor Anand was a gourmet cook by any stretch of the imagination.

"Do you remember how he maintained such a sunny disposition in front of the cameras despite facing a certain and sure death sentence?"

"Hmmmm … very brave of him, for sure," she replied after thinking for a while.

"I would probably put a bullet in my brain rather than go through chemotherapy hell like Dr. Pausch or Dr. Kalanithi."

She looked at him for a while and then responded: "Gabby Gifford's survived that."

Anand remained silent. Both remembered discussing the shooting in Arizona when it was in the news.

Anand was glad to be living in a time when wars were rare and India's wars were never the kind of total wars that countries in Europe had fought among themselves. Anand may have had reservations about joining the Air Force if that were to lead to his certain death by the age of 30. He would have perhaps chosen not to join the IAF – and he would have considered that decision to be a pragmatic, hard-headed decision. He didn't become an air force pilot because he wanted to be dead quickly; he joined because he thought it was a superb, challenging career that was in sync with his passions.

Anand did consider the career of a commercial pilot flying of an airline but flying fighters was an order of magnitude more challenging and more interesting from a pilot's perspective. Modern passenger jets – the Boeings and Airbuses – are such superb products of engineering that the pilots sitting in those aircraft are essentially 'supervising' the airplane's flight computers. The flying is mainly managed by the flight control software and the software is designed to keep the airplane flying well within its design tolerances. Such conservative principles have ensured that flying remains the safest way to travel from point A to point B.

The job of a captain in a commercial airline is to master the intricacies of the flight computers so that he can take over flying duties in case of some anomaly. In a fighter aircraft, the pilot flies

the plane while in a commercial airline the Autopilot does most
of the flying.

SCENE-12

Human Rights

"Theoretically, human rights exist everywhere. Practically, they exist on your side of the barbed wire."

Anand woke up with a blurry vision, feeling a sensation in his restrained hands. He could see the floor, with a dizzy head and a dehydrated soul. Someone was fiddling with the wire that had kept him tied to the sickening chair. He could hear footsteps approaching him. As he raised his brow to clear his vision, a man in a military uniform appeared. Physically taxed beyond the limit, he could barely keep his head aligned. The man's voice fell upon his ears. "Here. Drink some water," he said in a coarse masculine voice. Anand's brain suddenly registered an overwhelming sensation of freedom as he eased his hands in front of him. He was cut loose after a metaphorical century in that stinking room.

His arms had lost tolerance to resist anything. Being restrained like that for days had made them weak. Anand felt an excruciating pain burst through his forehead when he lifted them to grab that precious bottle of water. The pilot's inability to function normally caused the military *Jawan* to take a step forward. He brought the bottle's mouth closer to the dried and wrinkled lips. The first few drops morphed Anand's lips into a normal appearance. The subsequent gulps quenched his age-old deserted throat that struggled to produce voices. For the first time, Anand felt alive. His mind elevated towards normal functioning. Anand was now thinking.

"You need more?" the military man asked. Anand wanted more of it. He wanted to drink all the water in the world. His body shrieked for fresher water to survive. Though Anand nodded and refused. He raised his head slowly. The ray of light lit the manly figure in front of him. The badge on the man's chest read 'Hamid.' Before he could process anything else with his sluggish mind and fuzzy sight, he saw Hamid turn. A man in the whitish coat came closer to him. Anand's subconscious knew it was a doctor.

He heard the two men blabber before he fainted again. "He is way too dehydrated," Dr. Iqbal, an army Physician, gave his remark. "We need him in presentable shape, Dr.," Hamid said, "He needs to be in front of the camera soon." "Well...You give my team a few hours. We will make him walk and talk again," the shrink said. Hamid smiled. This answer probably gave him relief because he had felt for the poor Indian since the day of his capture. "Great!" Hamid remarked. "How is your daughter's wedding coming up?" he asked. "Girls, you see. Hahaha, nothing can be perfect for a big fat wedding for them...haha," The two men departed the room. The man who untied Anand left at last. He ensured that he made no mistake. He was as fanatic as his commanders and as fearful as a servant.

The door banged against the metal rim. In a few seconds, Anand opened up his eyes. He never fainted. He had played one of the 'Classic Anand' tricks from his playbook. With a deep breath, his mind raced. Anand was contemplating his captors' next move.

Why did they offer him water? Did they want him alive? Why was there a doctor? What was cooking? Anand began sawing his hands on the wooden edge of the chair. The rope was thick, and the edge was blunt. Yet, he summoned all his strength and sawed the rope. The friction strengthened with the man's persistence. Anand kept at it. Few slick lines of fume rose. A slight burning essence surrounded the chair, motivating Anand to keep sawing despite his muscles giving up. Then the metal door unflung itself again. Four tall figures entered the cellar.

Before they could realize it, Anand became limp again. "Why is he sweating?" one marshal asked. The doctor glanced at Anand's taxed body and placed the stethoscope on his chest suspecting nothing. "He seems to have a mild fever, hence, the sweat," he said as he gazed him over. "Well, we need to get going Doc…," said the marshal. The doctor nodded. At a moment's notice, the two guards untied Anand and held him up. Anand dangled between the two men who had failed to notice the half wretched string that tied the pilot to the chair.

A few hundred feet at the far end of the corridor that was studded with equally spaced cellars, some 20 in number, a military infirmary awaited the Indian officer. There was a lady assistant in the room that was doused with disinfectant and smelled strongly of formalin. The smell kicked Anand's mind into an active state, and he was almost energized for a moment. 'What are they doing now?' he thought as the guards lay him over a neat bed. "Get him in shape, Doc. We need to shoot him," the marshal ordered before leaving the personnel there. The word 'Shoot' clenched Anand's windpipe with hands of steel. Though, he regained his calm with rational thought. They weren't going to treat him well before putting a bullet in him. They were probably talking about shooting with a camera. His mind raced on the soft white bed.

He was awake now, and he could see the tin-made medical trays clinging together.

Lady shrink would take a look at him once in a while. Perhaps an Indian Air Force Officer perplexed her. Or maybe she was thinking about probable atrocities that her people might lay on him. Or maybe she was just fancying him for his mutton-chops. The pilot began forming a mental map of the facility, assessing facts and weaknesses that he could probably exploit. He wanted to escape badly. But he was also aware of the consequences that would befall him if he made a mistake. From every corner of the facility, muzzle ends of the Kalashnikovs protruded. Facing one of those was the last thing on his mind until he could 'secure' one for himself. "Sit up and lift your hands," the lady said curtly. Anand obeyed her.

She placed the stethoscope on his chest. Cold metal sent a tingling sensation through Anand's body, making him wonder if the woman's heart was as cold. With no empathy in her eyes, she moved the stethoscope to a few different spots on Anand's torso before removing them and keeping them aside. Anand saw her scribble over a register which she then handed to the doctor. The man had an oddly amiable vibe surrounding him. Though he was a doctor assisting the militia that had the capability of doing horrible things to Anand, which they had proved earlier frequently, Anand felt he had a secret soft side. He believed that the man knew of his deception back in the cellar and that the shrink had a notion of what he was up to.

The Doc grew closer to Anand, a small flashlight in his hand. "Now, open your mouth wide and layout your tongue," he asked. The doc chucked the torch on, its rays cutting a funnel of light in the well-lit room. Anand protruded his tongue. The doctor also checked his eyes for any unusual dilation of shrinkage. "Your vitals look fine," the doctor said. "Do you have pain, the severe kind, anywhere?" he asked with a weak smile. Anand looked elsewhere in the room before making eye contact with the doctor, took a deep breath, and said no. "You think you need a painkiller?" the doctor rolled another dice. Anand declined. He intermittently glared at the nurse standing in the background, adjusting his notch from time to time.

The doctor scribbled over the register one more time, turned around looking at it, and exited the room. As soon as he left, the nurse's calm demeanour wore off and a disgusting face replaced her fake one. She hated Anand's presence around her. The pilot read the room well, knowing of her strong dislike for him. He wasn't concerned though. Was it surprising? No. "Can I have some water, please?" he asked her softly. The nurse, startled at an unexpected request, stopped and looked at him. She looked right through Anand's soul.

"You have dared to ask me for water, huh?" her eyes grew bigger, almost bloodshot. Her tone remained hauntingly soft under her heavy breathing. The Indian pilot was a little perplexed at the unusual animosity of a nurse, who was a lady, a stranger, whom he could bet his eyes on about meeting for the first time in life. "I...I am..em sorry...?" Anand shot the obvious question with his insincere apology and deliberate pause. He looked directly in the eyes of the lady who was internally fuming with a raging tempest. She drew closer and Anand prepared for an unpredictable outcome. His vulnerability left him with limited choices. He had already eyed a surgical blade kept at about three feet from him to the right. 'Last resort,' he thought.

"You will burn in *Dozakh(hell)*, your generations will be

crippled forever," her voice growing louder into a roar. "Miss, I am sure we have nothing personal. I understand your position. But there is no rationale to hate me," Anand began his smooth ladies talk. "You killed my husband, bastard-" her throat became heavy, "You killed *Armaan*." Unable to fully process the woman's distress, Anand thought it'd be better to remain docile and listen to her than trigger her further. This was not the day either of them would bleed out the life through a surgical blade, he thought. With no apparent body movement, he asked the lady about the man he was talking about. "Armaan, Armaan, I get it. What happened to him?" he asked only to notice the rage shoot up in her eyes. The pilot's instincts told him she wanted him dead. Just like his instincts had saved his life on numerous flying missions, they were beckoning for the same now.

"You don't take his name from your foul mouth, mite..." She spat. "Armaan was my fiancé, the pilot martyred by your bullet. You will pay. I will make you pay," she said with her teeth grinding, sobbing.

***

The usual silence of Mr. Sharad Singh's office broke with the ringing telephone. A well-groomed man in his 50s, his frisking eyes peered from behind the glasses, hair perfectly parted-white as snow, and a diplomatic smile that took over his serious face at the most appropriate times. He picked up the receiver. "This is the Indian Consulate Office of Pakistan," he said, adjusting his notch. "Singh, Parekh here," the voice on the other end said. "Oh, well, hello Mr. Parekh. How may I assist the minister's office?" Singh said. "I need an update on the Pilot's situation. Parekh, the people are growing restless. What is the field team of yours doing?"

"Sir, I am being informed by the PAK Air Force that our pilot is safe."

"They used the word 'safe'?

"I am given to believe that, sir."

"What is the field force of yours doing? Any update?"

"Sir, they are trying to get in touch with the pilot. It is not easy I must tell. The public here is agitated too. But we are keeping it under the sheets as of now," Singh said.

Parekh sighed; his exhale was audible over the speaker. "Ok."

Singh paused, almost said something, then not. He said it anyway- "Sir, may I ask one thing?" "Sure. Go ahead." Singh widened his lips like a child, moisturized his lower lip, and asked, "Where is the international community on this matter? We can use some pressure here, especially given that the ball is not in our court!"

"Hmm...The ministry is working on that. You'll hear about that soon. Keep me updated," Parekh said. "Will do."

***

Anand had an escape plan, almost cooked, almost sane. But the emotionally distressed nurse was new trouble. He tried to talk his way out. "Look, I know how it looks. But I saw something else, an entirely different version of Armaan's death-Allah rest his soul-from what you are given to believe," he said looking into her red burning eyes. The nurse paused, pondered, and asked- "What do you mean? What version?"

"Yes, the true version. My version. Perhaps you can keep the knife down," Anand's eyes didn't let go of the shiny streak of the blade, "May, I ask your name, Miss?" he dared.

She looked at the blade, almost kept it, but changed her mind halfway. She decided it will be of use if she didn't like the story. Then turning her head towards him, she whispered, "Nafeesa."

Anand took a deep breath and exhaled. "Nafeesa- Valuable and Precious. No doubt. Nafeesa, I want to know first- What did your office tell you?" She snapped and raised the knife within a blink, ready to pierce his heart- "You don't get to be smart with me."

Anand, startled, raised his hands and almost screamed- 'No nonono...No, please no. What is with the knife lady?" He took charge of the dialogue the other way. "I mean can't you talk? Would it satisfy you to kill a bed-ridden guest who meant no harm?" he said.

For a moment, there was silence in the room. Then she explained, absorbing the reason Anand gave her.

"Armaan was killed in the plane you shot down. That is what everyone has seen. That is what I have been told. You shot his aircraft down, didn't you?" her reprehensible eyes glared at him. "Yes, I shot his plane. I believe it went down for the same reason…" "You son of a..." Nafeesa tightened her grip on the knife, her face expressionless "...But," Anand resumed. "It wasn't me who killed him." The nurse was perplexed, ready to discard any reason the pilot prepared for her. "He crashed. I was hiding on the ground. The village people caught him. They probably mistook him for an intruder. I was right there…" Anand's throat choked a little.

"What did...what did they do to him?"

For a moment, Anand fiddled with the bedsheet and gazed at it. "They...They lynched him. Beat him until he was unconscious. Shortly after that, I was caught."

Nafeesa's world shattered right there. It was hard for her to comprehend that her people would be the reason behind his Love's demise. She sat there, oblivious for the next few minutes until the doctor came in with an assistant.

The doctor's eyes, like the beads of glasses, revealed nothing behind them. He looked at the nurse. "Everything alright in here?" as he unpacked a capsule. She nodded lightly. He smiled and turned to Anand. "Here, take this." Anand's instincts came into play. "What is it?" "Medicine. To make you better again. You are going on camera," the Doctor said as his assistant motioned the 2-person camera crew inside the ward.

***

"Mr. Parekh? This is Singh speaking. I hope you have been watching TV. They are making him speak," Ambassador Singh informed the Indian Ministry of Foreign Affairs.

Power Corrupts

"In games of power and conspiracies, even your shadow is a suspect."

Since after a long time, Joseph and Leena had a solid lead at their disposal. To deduce the staff member's name who was supposedly killed was fairly easy. Investigators just had to ask the Chief jailer about such an incident where a staff member was beaten badly by the inmates. Though, Joseph had a long-shot suspicion of a person. He had noticed him before. A person hiding in plain sight. His nose smelled a solid clue after a long time. Sipping from his cup the mild honey-dew tea in his drawing-room, the new angle bombarded his brain with theories that would fit his suspicion.

Leena freshly awoke after a late-night sleep, joined Clinton Joseph in the drawing-room. She threw herself on the sofa and flip opened the laptop. "Got any sleep last night, boss?" Joseph glanced at her after a moment, came back to his senses. "Yeah... Just the right amount. 3.5 hours. You?" He asked slouching over the table, kept his empty cup in the pot. "Sufficient enough," she said with a smile. "Working on that cipher, huh?" he asked, floundering his pockets for another smoke. Leena glanced at him from behind her glasses and said yes.

"I think I am holding an important piece of the puzzle right now!" Joseph said, lighting his cigarette. Leena shifted her leg over the other and adjusted her spectacles giving all her attention to him. "We are moving in a few minutes. Back to Dolly," Joseph said, smoke dangling between his thin lips.

The SUV pulled again in front of the gate and an officer awaited the duo to greet them. Leena and Joseph stepped out. "Hello, we were expecting you. Chief is out on an emergency call," the tall, fair, and slim officer said. He shook Joseph's hand," I am Capt. Vijay Kumar Jetley," he said, "I'll be assisting you with your investigation today!"

"Very well, Captain!" Joseph said. "Actually, it won't take too long as far as I reckon. At any rate, we shall not disturb you for long," he gestured the young Captain with a rare smile. "Absolutely not, sir," Capt. Jetley said as he leads the duo inside the premises.

The trio sat in the Captain's office. The wooden desk was decorated with many perpetual machine toys amusing to watch. Leena watched them irresistibly. The Captain noted her attention and broke the ice. "How shall we get started, sir?" he asked. "Tea or coffee maybe!" Joseph crackled. Everyone laughed. "Absolutely," Jetley said. He rang the housekeeping bell. The old familiar buzz of the call bell made Joseph raise his brows.

"So, what is going to be the next step?" the Captain asked Joseph as he noted Leena's attention to the metal wheel rocking up and down on the glass rails kept on the table. Joseph took a deep breath. "Nothing much!" he muttered. "Nothing much. We just have to take a small trip nearby," he said. "A small trip?" the Captain raised his brows. "Yes," Joseph replied. A moment would have barely skipped before two light knocks came through the office door.

"Come in," Jetley said.

The door opened with a mild creak. A familiar old face peeked in first, disappeared, and then appeared with a tray of coffee and snacks. "Good morning, *Saheb*" Ram Bawa greeted the trio with a wide smile.

The Captain gave a formal smile and motioned the man to come over. Clinton Joseph didn't bother to make eye contact. Ram advanced towards the table, being docile enough to show respect to the room. He placed the coffee cups in front of each person.

"Anything else, *Saheb?*" he asked, crossing his hands in front of him, the tray covering his pelvis partially.

"We'll let you know!" Jetley said as he appeared busy with a pen and a notepad.

Ram Bawa bowed slightly and turned around to leave, his feet as silent as a leaf surfing the wind.

"You make a really good coffee!" Joseph exclaimed out of the blue. All eyes on him. Bawa stopped and turned around as he processed the fleeting remark. The Captain looked at Joseph casually and continued to write. Bawa smiled at the compliment. "Thank you, *Saheb!*" said he. "Oh! I'll truly be welcomed if you make this coffee at my house someday!" Joseph said with an invisible sneer. "I would be honored, sir," the man said. He turned around to go away before Clinton Joseph again remarked. "Why not now?" he asked.

For a moment, everybody thought it was an insincere proposition and Joseph was stretching the compliment too far. The coffee wasn't that great either, as told by Leena's expressions. "I am guessing you're having coffee after a long time, sir?" the officer asked. Everyone gave a formal laugh and Ram Baw stood at the door being a silent part of the conversation. "No, no. I am serious. Let us do it now," Clinton said. Leena quickly gauged the situation, realizing Clinton was on to something. She hinted at the Captain with an eye-gesture. "Okay...Bawa! Bawa, come back," Captain Jetley stood up. The man hurried towards the door again. "*Saheb* liked your coffee. Captain's right hand patted Bawa's shoulder. "He is insisting on going to his home. He is having some guests over. Please come!" The proposition was harmless. Even though Bawa wasn't sure of such an employment policy as per which the housekeeping staff could work for someone outside during the working hours, Captain Jetley's assurance worked well. "Ok, sir," he agreed.

Captain Jetley commanded the steering of Joseph's car, and Leena occupied the front driver-side seat. Bawa and Joseph sat in the middle row. The SUV Accelerated further up from Dolly 3. The road uphill was rough, and during the rainy season, it took more than just skilled drivers to push a car up. It took nerves of steel to drive a vehicle that big fast on the bumpy elevation. Captain took brief note of the slush hitting the rear glass as the SUV roared up a narrow, steep pathway in 4x4.

A moment of silence prevailed in the car, and Ram Bawa's eyes rolled on either side. At this point, he wondered whether his coffee was that special. Jetley kept glancing at the rearview with sharp narrow eyes. From behind the palm trees on the roadside emerged a squeaky looking house. Its wooden structure was infested with green moss and strands of white fungus, though the house looked habitable. At the sight of the tragic looking yet beautiful looking building, Bawa lost his nerve.

The four souls deboarded and advanced to the front door. "Uh...is this your house, *Saheb?*" Bawa's meek voice broke. Nobody talked, they kept walking. The stone steps lead to the wooden porch. Leena and Jetley lead the way, followed by Bawa who was accompanied by Joseph. Joseph wound his right hand over Ram Bawa's shoulder and lit a cigarette. The servant almost flinched but didn't. "Let's take a walk before you dazzle us once again with your culinary skills," he said as he motioned Bawa to move with him.

"Why are we here?" Captain Jetley whispered. Leena looked around, registering every detail about the property. "I think we are going to find a surprise here," she said. "Surprise?" Captain was puzzled. He saw Joseph taking Bawa for a walk behind the house through a narrow muddy trail lined with weeds. Leena opened the door and invited the Captain in. "Whose house is this, anyway?" Jetley asked. "We'll meet the owner in just a while," she replied with a calm demeanour if knowing what was about to happen.

Moments passed. It was a loud crack, perhaps a gunshot, that rang through the valley behind the abandoned wooden house. Leena and Jetley went running outside. Following the trail which Bawa and Joseph followed earlier, the duo reached a small open farm behind the house. Joseph stood there with the gun pointed at something on the ground. It was Ram Bawa. Joseph noted Leena and kept staring at the ground. "What happened, sir?" Asked Captain Jetley, already holding a .45 Colt in the hand, tight grip ready to shoot. "Walk over here," Clinton Joseph motioned.

The duo made their way over the knee-high grass and was

instantly repulsed by a rotting stench. The body had partially decayed. Chunks of composting flesh hung from the bones. Maggots crawled out of the eye-sockets and everyone wanted to throw up. "You had one of your staff members away on the holiday, right?" Joseph asked. Captain looked at him and then at the body. "Is he…? is….Oh damn!" was all he could say. "And, here we have the implant with us. Ram Bawa. The docile servant keeper, the extraordinary coffee maker, the implant," Joseph said as he grinned. "Let's talk over a cup of coffee, Mr. Bawa!" he said, pulling the man up by the collar.

The engine roared, and the SUV rattled its way downhill.

Pray for Truth

"Truth does not always come out. Sometimes, you have to pray"

"We have a lot many questions for you. We want you to answer them truthfully. If you lie or try to deceive us, the more pain you will endure. Let us do this the easy way," Captain Jetley instructed Bawa handcuffed to a metal chair. It was a small abandoned cottage, a few miles uphill from Dolly 3. Joseph had advised interrogating Bawa outside of the facility to keep any suspicion down. Bawa could accompany other implants in the facility itself.

Wooden walls and wooden floor sheltered the cottage. A few cobwebs dangled from the ceiling corners. The furniture was scattered, stale and hot air asked for the windows to be opened, and there was probably a dead rodent somewhere close. *Cling! Cling!* Bawa's steel handcuffs brushed against the metal tubes of the creaky old chair. Ram Bawa didn't attempt to escape even once. Though his restlessness grew and Leena figured that his calm demeanor was falling apart. It was just a matter of push that would make the man talk, so Leena thought.

Joseph looked at Jetley. The Captain then pulled out a small black Korean-made Tape Recorder. Joseph dragged another creaky metal chair and sat face to face with the handcuffed man. Silence prevailed for a moment, and Joseph leaned back. "Leena, can you get me some water, please?" Leena, at once, went away to fetch a glass of potable water. Jetley assumed a standing position behind Bawa, his arms crossed across his chest.

"Look at me, pal," Joseph's cold voice directed at Bawa, who was stealing away his eyes. "Look at me. It's going to be very simple for you. Just tell us the whole story like a book. You walk away," he said. Ram Bawa clenched-unclenched his fists, sweat broke out on his face and shone like little pearls on his forehead. Leena came in. She extended the water bottle to Joseph, who took it without moving his eyes from Bawa. Leena assumed a guarding position by the wooden door that had two small holes. Two light rays funneled through the sparkling dust microns afloat in the air.

"I...I am scared, *Saheb*. I don't know what is happening. That body, you all...I am terrified *Saheb*," Bawa's voice shivered. Seeing no reactions, he continued. "Why have you apprehended me? I am just a servant. I serve. Now I am cuffed to a chair. Why *Saheb?*" his voice quivered, his eyes like little reservoirs of water.

Joseph rolled his eyes up, exasperated. He took a deep breath, pacified his hairline. "So, you want to do this the difficult way, huh?" he said. "Okay. Difficult it is then." He stood up, took out his car keys. Bawa couldn't swallow the fear anymore. "What have I done to upset you, Saheb?" he broke into tears. "I was just taking a walk with you and we stumbled across the body."

Joseph steadied Bawa's left-hand fingers. He then put the key-blade perpendicularly between Bawa's middle finger and index finger. The blade ran below the one and above the other. "We call this the 'Twisted Key' in our language. Chinese Government uses it on the political prisoners and they don't remain political anymore, haha," he said. He lit another cigarette. Bawa's voice broke out again. "*Saheb, saheb...*Please. I am innocent."

For the next 6-7 minutes, which seemed like an eternity in that wooden cottage, Bawa's distressed voices failed to breach the shabby wooden walls. His fingers, red and swollen, sent bone-chilling waves of pain across his conscious mind.

"Perhaps that would be sufficient!" Joseph looked into Bawa's eyes as he removed the car key from between his fingers. Bawa could barely breathe. Damaged tissue shone through his fingers along with the blue bruises. Leena and Jetley held their positions. "I'll be more specific with you. You have to be specific in your answers. Fair terms," said Joseph.

"How did the body get there? Who killed the man and why?" Joseph waited for the man to respond. "I...I.," Bawa mumbled and the next thing he experienced was Joseph's flying hand across his face. "Try to remember faster…"

Breaking Bawa into telling the truth was difficult than what the trio had expected. Soon, the sunset bought cricket chirps and hooting of the owl into the cabin. 6 hours of painful torture proved to be futile. True, Bawa was scared. But that was it. He never opened his mouth. Jetley took his turn at him, punched him, threatened him, kicked him. He didn't break. Leena played mind games with him; he didn't break.

The dark blue sky had only a few minutes of light left. Joseph stood at the doorway, leaned against one edge. Jetley sat at the footstep in the porch and Leena sat in the chair, staring constantly at handcuffed Bawa who was bleeding from his mouth, nose and was dehydrated. Everyone was sweaty. The room that earlier smelled like stale air now smelled like a pool of sweat.

Joseph turned around, looked at Leena and Captain Jetley. He took a few steps towards Bawa, who seemed to be content with his invincibility. Ram Bawa kept insisting on his innocence. Even Leena began doubting the man of any fishy involvement. Joseph stood beside Leena's chair. "Remember that old case of Delhi Blasts, Leena?" he asked.

"Yeah. What about it?"

"Our interrogation method?"

Leena's head turned towards Joseph.

"Sir?... Would that?"

Joseph looked at her. Jetley came over. He whispered in Joseph's ears. "We might already be in trouble. We have apprehended him illegally and human rights will blow us to pieces in the Court of Justice. We can't do this on our own, besides..." Joseph turned to him, said nothing. "One last try, if you may?" Clinton Joseph asked for the Captain's consent. The Captain said nothing and went out.

"Leena. Bring me a cotton cloth, a T-shirt would also do," Joseph said. Leena did the same.

The metal chair creaked once again as Joseph lowered himself on it. He had an unsettling smile on his face. "Well. You are tough. No doubt." He lit another cigarette.

"Let us test you for the last time," he said. He motioned over to Leena, who assumed a position behind Bawa. She then put a cotton T-shirt over Bawa's face. Perplexed, he flung and gasped for air. Leena tightened a nylon noose around the neck to fasten the cloth. Bawa struggled like a wild game trapped in the snare. He shouted, moved wildly, jerked his legs, and begged *Saheb* to let him go.

Leena then brought in a metal jerrycan filled up to brim with cold water. "Let it roll," Joseph said. As Ram Bawa flung around the chair, restrained, Leena unloaded the cold water onto him. The first few seconds were numb, then the real pain began. Bawa was drowning inside the T-shirt, wrapping his head. He kicked the floor hard enough to break his ankle. A shriek ensued and Leena removed the hooding cloth over Bawa's head with a jerk.

Joseph took the jerrycan and began operating the scene himself. He repeated waterboarding Bawa's hood until he was too tired to breathe. Bawa almost lost his consciousness. It was time to talk, and Bawa knew it. "Let us discuss something new, apart from what you've already told us which is nothing," Joseph said. Joseph untied Ram Bawa's hands, inserted a cigarette into his mouth, and lit it. "This will help," he said as he sat in the chair again.

The old wooden cottage was immersed in silence for another hour. Bawa talked. He gave the team all the outlines they were looking for. The finer details were evident now.

The front door opened and Captain Jetley shoved the new prisoner into the back seat of the SUV. He cuffed him to the grab handle and went back to the porch where Leena and Joseph stood. "Revelations, huh! Water made the man talk like the radio," Jetley remarked.

"What now, sit?" Leena asked Joseph. He kept looking at Bawa sitting in the car. "Well, we now know the information he has given is true to an extent," said Joseph. "I am compelled to believe the same. I got the meaning of *Liba*, at least," Leena said. "You did? What did it mean?" asked Joseph. "*Liba* is a mythical feminine figure, an extra-ordinary beauty that one can only meld-with in heaven," she said. "Remember that painting in Khaled's cell?" Leena asked. "Yes," Joseph nodded. "The story is finally unraveling," she said.

Joseph smiled. The same smile that was a tell about Joseph holding a big secret. This smile of his only surfaced when he played Sudoku and won. "What is it? What did you figure?" Leena grew curious. Jetley closed-in with sharp ears.

"Bawa told us about a big terror training camp somewhere in Pakistani territory. But he still maintains that he doesn't know the location, that he is just another foot-soldier, right?" he said. "I just had to confirm this. The last piece of the puzzle that was bothering me."

"Last piece?" Leena asked.

"Remember the cipher I gave you on the first day of your report? *4 Strides to the North, 73 strides to the East, our 1,24,000?*" Joseph asked to which Leena nodded yes.

"Well. We have the location of the terror-training camp now. 73 Degrees East, 4 Degrees North. 1,24,000 is a symbolic number, a dramatic touch. It signifies many recruits under training for a big strike. 1,24,000 points towards the number of Prophets... Prophets, huh!"

"Well, well! This is the big attack then!" Leena said, looking at Joseph and Jetley.

The trio sped downhill in the SUV as Joseph connected with

the Home Ministry.

Based on the intel, a few days later, the Indian Government decided to take a preemptive approach, a daring step overlooking all international diplomatic relations. Above all, it was an act defying all stances India ever took in history.

'Operation 'Bandar' (Monkey)' was given a green light. In the wee hours of 26 February 2019, 12 heavily armed Mirage 2000 aircraft of the Indian Air Force flew towards the Khyber Pakhtunkhwa region, beyond the Indian border into Pakistan.

On the target screen of the Indian aerial warriors lied one target- Jaish-e-Mohammad Terrorist Training Camp. Within minutes, the squadron of Mirage aircraft breached the Pakistani airspace, dropped the bombs, and returned to safety.

The camp was destroyed and this act by Indian Air Force made headlines throughout the International media. Pakistan grew restless.

Following this, Pakistan alerted its Air Force. Indian armed forces increased air surveillance and patrolling across its airspace. It was during this period, post the Balakot air-strike, when Wing Commander Anand fell into the Pakistani hands.

Death and Truce

"A failed truce is the one that prevails after millions of war deaths. A successful truce is the one that arrives just before the millionth death."

"Yes. I need to talk to Mr. Rashed. Now!" Parekh said in a firm voice that dominated the listener's ears. "Um. Okay. Hold on while I transfer the line, sir," the lady from Pakistan's Office of Foreign Affairs said in a meek voice. Parekh waited, carefully planning his words. He was deemed an expert in conducting transactions and negotiations involving international delegations. This negotiation was dear to him. He had been in touch with Clinton Joseph and his team.

The other side of the phone came alive in a few seconds. *"Salam-Aleykum, Parekh Miya.*

It has been a while since I talked to an old acquaintance. When was it...Uh...Last *Ramadan*I believe...Haha? Tell me. What brings your attention to me?" the man with the heaviest voice in the universe spoke up. He was no other than the immediate advisor to Pakistan's Prime Minister, General Maqdoom Rashed.

"Indeed. It has been a long time. How about I invite your office to a grand treat in New Delhi this Diwali, huh?" Parekh replied with equally vehement diplomacy. A moment of silence ensued. "Absolutely. I shall hope so. Haha," Maqdoom gave another laugh. Parekh wanted to cut to the chase. But upsetting Maqdoom only meant a delay and Maqdoom's temper was 'Asia famous.'

"My friend Maqdoom. I hope you and your family are in the best of their health. I have a reason I called you. It is regarding Anand," Parekh said in an amiable yet firm voice. "Anand? Anand who? The Bollywood actor? haha...I apologize, but I have no news of him. Sorry!" said Maqdoom. Parekh understood that he wanted to waste time. He took charge of the conversation. "Haha. That one never gets old," Parekh said (not really understanding the joke because of its lack of humor). "Though, not the Bollywood actor. The Pilot, I suppose," he said. "Oh! He belongs to you?" Maqdoom said. A moment of silence. Then Parekh said yes. "Well, what all he says is- *I am not supposed to tell you that.* We don't know who this man is, Parekh," said Maqdoom Rashed, his sinister side making lurches in his voice from deep within.

"Mr. Maqdoom. I understand the confusion you might be in. I assure you; he is our decorated officer. And, we want him released immediately," Parekh said, his amicable tone lost way behind. "Oh, so you say. But he could be Mossad (Secret Intelligence), CIA (Central Intelligence Agency), who knows? We found him loitering around on our side of the country, Parekh. He can be a threat to us. Now, I shall assure you. Pakistani court will seek justice. The wrong-doer shall be penalized. If he is proved to be innocent, he is free to go." Maqdoom did not seem to be in a mood to negotiate.

"Do you have terms?" Parekh asked.

"Terms, haha. My dear Indian friend. We do not enter terms with those beneath us…"

At this point, Parekh's intuition fired up. He knew if Pakistan was unwilling to put forward any terms of negotiation for the release of the pilot despite releasing his video on media, he will be killed. Parekh thought that the Pakis will make it look like an accident. No accountability, no deniability. The way Pakistan has been functioning for decades.

"Okay, Mr. Maqdoom. Here is the deal from 'those beneath you.' Within a few minutes, a few of the terrorist camps located deep within the Pakhtunkhwa region will be obliterated out of existence. India will not even need international support to justify anything. Fine, keep the pilot with yourself. Be ready to allocate a hefty budget to dig some good number of graves," Parekh switched to his classic warning mode.

"Moreover, it will take Pakistan another century to rebuild its image worthy enough to secure loans from the World Bank if we expose your Prime Minister's 'freelancing' activities. If you think you can beg uncle Sam, know that USS Nimitz is floating in the Indian Ocean, begging us to launch a strike. Uncle Sam gave you the F-16s. Now he aches for Indian friendship. Give the Prime Minister my deepest regards. Our delegation will be waiting for Wing Commander Anand at the point of your choice," said Parekh. "And, one more thing. We will think of inviting you to New Delhi next year," he said as he hung up the phone.

***

The cellar gate flung open. Anand was having tea, quite unbelieving of the treatment he was getting for the past few hours.

There were no beady-eyed officers, there were no questions, there were no threats. Still, Anand had its reservations about the enemy that was so unpredictable and on all the occasions, utterly ruthless. He knew that the video was shot for real. Yet, he was doubtful as to whether it was broadcasted. Deep down within his subconscious, he thought the act of shooting the video was another mind trick being played on him. 'What could they want? Why the video?' the question kept ringing a bell in his mind as he slurped the last sip from his *kullad* (earthen cup).

He heard multiple footsteps approaching his cellar. The door creaked open and a new face stood by the entrance. Behind the face stood a feminine figure. "Mr. Anand. How are you feeling now? Better, I hope. I am Fawad Al-Shabab, secretary of the Prime Minister's office," the man dressed in a grey suit with a smile constantly lightning his face said. He acted as if he was greeting a long-time acquaintance, an old lost friend.

Anand was a little surprised to see a diplomat for the first time since his capture. He was feeling at ease after a long time. "How are you feeling, Anand? I have a lady officer with me. She works for the Indian Embassy in Pakistan. She is here to give you a crucial piece of information," Fawad said. "It is strongly recommended that you listen to her. If I were you, I'd listen to her," he said, motioning over the lady to come forward.

She took a few steps forward and stood in front of the seated Anand. She had black hair, boasted a figure of a young mother, fair, and had green eyes that could look through a person. Her lips were the slices of precious red, and her face resembled the famed Iranian beauties. She spoke to Anand in the most feminine voice ever. "Hello. I am Tarannum Kaur. I am a foreign relations officer at the Indian Embassy of Pakistan. I am here to talk to you about your status in Pakistan,".

"Well, I am glad. Can I see your ID Card, please?" Anand asked. She hung the card outside her right coat pocket and displayed it to the pilot. After gazing for a moment, Anand said, "Hmm, looks legit. Haha. So, what is going on? You can tell me the story."

***

It was like a festival. There were guards of the border patrol units, decorated, standing with high heads at Wagha Border. The place hadn't witnessed such a sea of TV Journalists, freelance reporters, onlookers, security forces, and international delegations for a long time. There was a hint of stress in the air, which was surprisingly liberating.

At any given moment, all the eyeballs were fixated at the other end of the Wagha Border. A few hours earlier, Pakistan announced the condition-free release of Wing Commander Anand. The moment was no less than the festival of Diwali for the nation.

Anand's team of squadron leaders was present in their full uniform along with the IAF Spokesperson. "Pakis spared themselves some more kaboom-boom," Squadron Leader Param joked as the team waited for Anand's arrival. "Yeah? Air Marshal would never have given the exfil-mission a green flag," Mrityunjai sounded disappointed. Wg. Cdr. Rustom Paniwala couldn't help but overhear the young officer's chatter. He was well aware of their 'proposal' to Air Marshal.

Rustom turned around and looked at the boys. "Squadron Leader Mandal. You need to respect the system and its protocols," he said. "We had the Indian Navy on standby all this time to carry out an aggressive rescue strike if necessary," Rustom said. "Anand is not just important to you. He is a national asset."

BACK IN KASHMIR, Leena switched on the television. Joseph sat there on the couch. Leena offered him a pack of Marlboros. "I think I am done with these babies for a while. I call quits," he said. Leena was flabbergasted for a moment. She smiled and said, "Oh my! You think you know a man, huh," feeling happy for Clinton Joseph.

Leena increased the Television's volume as the news anchor announced-"Wing Commander Anand is now arriving at the Indian side of the LoC through Wagha Border. Initial reports claim that he looks well, and within a few minutes, the IAF will receive him."

"Let us head out for a coffee," Leena proposed. "Well, I was thinking about this fine English Malt that Dutta gave us," Joseph said.

Welcome home! Good to be back

There is a public persona we maintain and there is a private version of us. In public, we might be putting up an act – trying to convey to others a certain image about us. Some people like to boast in public about all the connections to powerful people they have – this politician or that powerful officer and so forth. Some people try to project an image of how successful they are in life. Many people make a career out of being 'success coaches.' Admittedly, if you want to teach others about how to succeed in life, you have to first convince others that you are super successful. In most cases, such projections are a mirage – if there was a formula to be successful, then everyone would follow that formula and everyone would become successful. Usually what gurus promise is to reveal a secret and that only a few can become successful by following their formula. This is contradictory – if it is a formula, then everyone should be able to follow it. If only a few can succeed, then maybe they would have anyhow succeeded whether with or without the help of a coach.

Anand thought about the various religious figures and godmen who keep prospering in India. Many end up in jail – and then others appear on the stage fooling yet more people.

There was something in humans which yearned for someone who would give all the answers and solutions which created a scope for demagogic political leaders, religious charlatans, and fraudulent business people who might promise to double and quadruple your wealth in a few months.

After Pakistan released Anand at the Wagah border, he made his way home amid much fanfare. He maintained a stoic face while in public. Once he reached the Research and Referral Hospital for preliminary medical evaluation, he met his parents, Nandini, and the kids. Everyone kept their emotions in check as there were people present and not much privacy was available.

Anand and Nandini locked eyes for a moment and exchanged a brief smile which conveyed to both that everything was going to be alright. Both knew that the detailed 'debrief' between husband and wife would have to wait for a while.

Anand was not one given to extravagant displays of emotion and aviators are anyway taught to maintain their cool under pressure.

In Anand and Nandini's case, both being pilots, their baseline was a little different than that for ordinary civilians in terms of what constituted a real crisis. They were not the kind to worry in a hurry – say, over a trifling fender bender incident in Bengaluru or Chennai traffic.

There are talkers and there are doers. Aviators like Anand belonged squarely in the group of doers. These aviators are not given to exorbitant displays of triumphalism – this goes all the way to aviators like Neil Armstrong, Michael Collins, and Buzz Aldrin.

This is quite a contrast from the ornate displays by sportspersons on football fields, cricket fields, and elsewhere.

Anand had been thrust into the public eye unexpectedly.

As it turns out, there are no quick fixes and there are no magic wands that can be waived to solve all the problems that beset the world. Anand understood this and understood the enormous strides our civilization has made. We live in a world that is immeasurably better than even the world of a century ago. Humans have walked the Earth for about 200,000 years out of which recorded history spans a mere couple of thousands of years or so. Humans were hunter-gatherers for most of our history. It's only very recently that people learned agriculture and farming and cooking food and living in communities. They formed nations and developed identities and allegiances and learned to fight on behalf of those identities and allegiances. This is somewhat unique among animals – no other animals define themselves based on their citizenship. This is indicative of the capability of humans to create and identify abstract concepts – this is mostly good and sometimes bad. After all, we are the only species that knows to think and wonder about our place in the universe and wonders about where it all came from or how it all came to be. We wonder about what is the ultimate meaning of life. No other animals do.

Time was a fascinating concept and reading and thinking about deep time was a hobby Anand indulged in. Anand believed that scientific ideas and scientific concepts can be conveyed in a non-technical language without using mathematics and then every educated person should try to acquaint themselves with as much of the latest scientific developments as possible.

Not that Anand thought he would have been better off as a physicist or professor or academic.

Domino State

"A nation's integrity rests upon the integrity of states. One weak link can corrode it all."

A few weeks later.

A lady in her 40s with the appearance of a much younger woman stood behind Parekh with a tea-saucer. She looked at the man she had been married to for the past 27-years, then looked at the television screen and the newspaper that tried to fly under the ceiling fan. Parekh was asleep, lost in a peaceful wonderland. His wife adored the look on his face and was relieved to see him relax. She placed the saucer on the table over which Parekh's legs rested. She then placed her legs cautiously down on the table and shook him slightly. Parekh woke up, recognized Dimpy's face, and smiled.

Dimpy assumed her place on the chair placed adjacent to Parekh's couch, kept staring at him. "What?" Parekh asked, a little shy, as he lifted the teacup. Dimpy smiled and said- "I can't remember the last time I saw you at peace. I can finally be at ease now, huh!"

Parekh nodded playfully and chose not to utter any word. But he did anyway. "Where is Jigna?" he asked. "Thank God! You remember your daughter's name!" Dimpy's sarcasm widened his smile. Parekh had always adored the way his wife threw tantrums, taunts, and demands at him. If it wasn't for her, he would have given up on life long ago. "I know my children's names. This is the least I can do for you, haha," he joked. Dimpy threw a cushion at him. "She is out for her Aero-modelling classes," Dimpy said. She suddenly started touching his feet with her soft, white bare feet. "Got date plans for tonight?" she asked. Parekh looked into her eyes, kept the teacup aside, pulled her closer. "Dear…" he had just begun, and the cell phone rang.

The eye-contact never broke and Parekh picked up the call. Holding Dimpy in one hand, the cell phone in the other, he proceeded. "Hello." "Jai Hind, Mr. Parekh. Gopeshwar this side," the man said. "Yes, Gopeshwar, what do you have for me?" "Sir, urgent meeting at the Prime Minister's Office. 12:30 pm today." "This is regarding…?" "I am not sure, it's classified." "Okay. I'll be there," said Parekh as he disconnected the call and gave Dimpy a passionate kiss.

"You can't stay sane, can you?" She asked him with a smile. Parekh nodded no and told her about the meeting, which was to commence three hours later.

"Better get ready, busy man," Dimpy said, looking at him like a needy child who wouldn't let him go if heavens were with her.

***

Prime Minister's Office, 7-Race Course, New Delhi

The heavy, black iron door swung open and four Special

Protection Group officers scanned Parekh's vehicle. The boundary wall surrounding the PM House was 8-feet high, and every corner had a manned observation tower. The black Indian-made sedan entered the gate under the watch of armour-piercing muzzles.

A few more cars entered and the front gate was soon sealed. The silence at the PMO's gate is a rarity, which is otherwise under a constant watch from the paparazzi. It seemed that only a select few individuals had the notion of this gathering, and all of them were inside now.

As the invited delegation entered the house, Prime Minister's Personal Secretary, Mr. Rehan Daruwala escorted them to the conference room. The conference room had a large elliptical table big enough to accommodate 30 people at once. With each blue cushioned chair, a water bottle, a headset, and a microphone were placed. Every chair had the name-badge designation to point to the intended person.

The delegation soon assumed its place alongside the conference table. Daruwala switched ON the projector screen and made an announcement- "Prime Minister will join us in exactly 5-minutes. Mr. Clinton Joseph will lead the meeting."

Parekh looked around and saw all the familiar faces. Before the group could indulge in talks among themselves, the PM entered the room.

Without looking at every individual face as he walked in, the Prime Minister swiftly positioned himself at the table head. "Gentlemen!" he acknowledged everyone. By the time his charismatic demeanour, confident gait, and bright face lit with grit engulfed the room's vibe, his soldiers were already sitting straight and attentive.

"You may start the discourse, Joseph," the Prime Minister said. Joseph stood up, looked everyone in the eye to greet them, and began.

"Thank you everyone for being here on time. The matter is urgent," he said as he moved towards the projection screen with a small remote between his fingers.

"Memories of the recent national events are fresh in our minds. And so, our Prime Minister and his advisors have put forward a proposal," said Joseph.

Every eye and every ear in the room was focused on Joseph.

Joseph looked at the PM as if seeking his approval. He then said, "The idea is to take J&K under the direct control of the Indian constitution…"

A few consecutive seconds of silence was met by perplexed and questioning faces. This, the proposers had expected. "I know there are questions. Let's sort it out," said Joseph.

Minister of Culture and Indigenous Development, Shakti Devegowda interrupted the discourse with his doubt. "I don't think we can do anything about Article 370. It is a constitutional clause granting J&K the power of an autonomous state."

Head of Minorities Union, Arshad Sulemani, added his views that there is no need for such a move at all. A few others backed him on a similar line of thought. Joseph stood there listening, waiting for them to gather some patience and listen to the proposal. A few heads remained silent, however.

The Prime Minister's shadow could be seen standing up. In a moment, all the whispering and confusion were gone. All eyes were on him now. "Gentlemen!" He said. "Let's listen to what Joseph has to say. I never thought the abrogation of Article 370 would be met with friction. Still, please allow the man to continue."

Sulemani seemed a little flipped by the idea. The other opposing seniority was silent now.

"So, as I was saying," Clinton Joseph proceeded, "The plan is to abrogate 370 and establish the Constitutional order in the state. Now, questions…"

"Have we talked to the residents of the state? Do they want 370 to be removed?" Sulemani's cynical words were out.

"And, what about the insurgents? We don't know where the loyalty of those people lies…!" Devegowda said.

"Those people??" Prime Minister said, removing his glasses, placing them on the table. "Those are our people, Mr. Devegowda. And they are vulnerable because of the state's autonomy."

It was as if Devegowda was condemned by the supreme leader of the clan and was now being frowned upon by everyone. Devegowda took shelter in the arms of silence.

Sulemani decided to take advantage of the awkward situation to position his point. "But, Honourable PM, what purpose would Abrogation of 370 solve? I mean, we can use pressure groups to direct the J&K Govt. We have military footing there, and…"

"Mr. Sulemani," the PM's voice silenced his objection. "J&K is not just a matter of pride. People need the Central Government's rule over there. Indians have suffered lifelong fatigue of tyranny there. They are caught between religion, communities, militancy, fear, insurgency, human rights, and patriotism. We can't allow this to be endured by our people there."

Silence in the conference room ensued.

Joseph took the cue and continued to support the Prime Minister's argument. "This is a high-time, gentlemen. Article 370 was a mistake. Now is the time to correct it!"

"Mistake??" Sulemani objected.

"Yes, a mistake. Don't you think a separate dominion state has already split apart Indians and Kashmiris? Don't you think every Indian should be able to move about in that state freely, establish property and businesses to boost the economy? Don't you want Kashmiri youth to be a part of the rapidly progressing mainstream India? Most importantly, don't you think the residents of J&K deserve human rights and freedom just like any other Indian?" Joseph argued as he walked to and fro in front of the projector.

"I assume we have an internal motion of confidence on the subject," Gopeshwar underlined the discourse with a spark of humour.

"Joseph, brief the gentlemen about the execution of the plan. The bill will be passed by the President's order soon. Keep this under wraps for as long as you can," said the Prime Minister as he stood staring out the window into his lush green garden.

War and Freedom

"Wars are expensive. Freedom is invaluable. That is the greatest dilemma."

August 2019

It was a lavish room, of the likes of the colonial royalty. A room large enough to house the most exquisite furniture, antiques, rare paintings, and hunting-trophies. The wall-decor gave a lavish vibe that was intense enough to put the rich of New Delhi to shame. To an outsider, it would have been instantly evident that the place belonged to a person or a family known for their bon vivant existence.

On the heavily studded blood-red sofa, that had golden embroidery along its edges, sat a lady- her head covered with a religious hijab, clothes of a monotonous dark streak, jet-black mascara lining her big round eyes, and face as white as freshly brewed milk. The entrance to the room was guarded by two *Pathan* men, AK-47 muzzles protruding from the back of their shoulders.

The lady's cell phone rang. She glanced at the screen for a

while, sighed, and swiped the green button. "Hmm," the lady hummed. "*Salam-aaley-kum,*" an old, tipsy sounding voice broke on the speaker from the other side. "What is it now?" the lady stood up and walked towards the large windowpane that stood between her and a valley decorated with pine trees and junipers draped in morning dew.

"Our setup was compromised by your government. You still cannot take a stand. And you ask, what is it now? Huh," the old voice cracked. The lady kept mum, stared out the window. "*Miya,* I know this land better than you and your ancestors. *Insha-allah,* let me do as I see fit," she said. "Hahaha, *Mufti Bibi,* I understand the depth of your mind pretty well. I just hope…" and the voice went blank. "Hello, hello," Bibi Nafeesa Mufti tried to connect. "Hello, *Aka*…Hello," she became frantic as the cell phone went mute.

Grinding her teeth in frustration, she flipped the cell phone away on the table and went inside the room. A guard autonomously picked her cell phone up, checked it out, and placed it on the glass-top table. Suddenly, he was summoned by the lady. He ran inside the room. Bibi Mufti stood there staring at the TV static. She turned towards him, anger bubbling on her face.

"What are you looking at *Murkhaan,*" she grinned. Adam Khan stood there, bowed in submission. "Go check why the TV is not working," Nafeesa Bibi shouted. Adam Khan bowed and left.

The static on the TV screen suddenly vanished and a blue screen appeared. A text ticker scrolled along the screen's width. *This is an emergency broadcast. All communication services of your area have been temporarily suspended. Remain calm. Local authorities and governments will assist you.*

It was as if Nafeesa Mufti's legs were paralyzed. Every muscle fiber in her body signalled stress, and her mind screamed of a massive change taking place in her state, without her knowledge. The state where she ruled as the Chief Minister for more than a decade was under the influence of an unknown force. Though, the nature of that force was well known to Nafeesa Bibi.

She gathered her calm, strode to the drawing-room, and ordered her guards to prepare the car. Nafeesa then grabbed a satellite phone from behind the white tea-set kept over the clock cabinet. Frantically, she dialled the only contact she had saved in the phone's memory. "Salaam, Dilshad," she spoke in an agitated tone. "Dilshad, are you there?" Post the silence of a few seconds, the voice on the other side finally opened up. "Waaley-kum-asalam, Bibi," the man said. His voice was that of a young Kashmiri man.

"Do you know what is happening?" Nafeesa asked.

"I only know what you know. I have no clue, Bibi," Dilshad said.

"Cell phones, TV, internet, all gone..." Nafeesa grew restless.

"Jamal told me that he saw some movement at night, at the city's entrance."

"What movement, *Murkhaan?*" she asked.

"Military, Bibi, military. *Hindustani fauji*s here," Dilshad said.

"No, it can't be. I am the CM and there has been no news, no update from the center," Nafeesa Mufti said.

"I only know what I am telling you."

"*Allah,* what is cooking? Dilshad, time to take control," she said.

"*Hukum,* Nafeesa Bibi."

"How fast can your boys take action?"

"At a moment's notice, Bibi!"

"I want each of them covering their area. Give them a free hand. Stones, fire, bullets, whatever it takes. You understand?"

"Freehand? But Bibi, what if they come across the *Fauj?*"

"Ask them to cover everything on their stupid smartphones. As many videos as they can generate as evidence of the suppression. Now don't throw a single more 'if' or 'but' at me."

And she hung up the phone and laid her weight on the couch. "*Bibi-Jaan,* the car is ready," a guard announced. Nafeesa moved towards the entrance giving no further thought. The pairs of boosts and her sandals trotted towards the compound where her white Toyota Camry stood. Two other Jeeps were ready to escort the CM of the state. The situation was tensed, the state was under a strange influence. Events got even stranger when Nafeesa and the guards saw three military trucks and a few jeeps of the Indian Border Security Force pulling right across the main-gate of the CM House.

In the moments of shock and awe, she noticed a white Ambassador car pulled by the trucks as the armed company took a stance in front of the house. A man with a dark handlebar moustache, sunshades, and height that resembled Napoleon Bonaparte appeared from the backdoor of the car. As he directed his steps towards Mufti, the armed BSF personnel secured the perimeter of the house. Nafeesa Mufti was well aware of the Indian National Security Advisor, Vineet Jamwal.

"Ms. Mufti, I hope we haven't interrupted you in your undertakings. I believe you were leaving for some urgent work, is it?" Jamwal said, removing his goggles. Nafeesa stood like a statue. "Yes," she mumbled as she tried to establish the eye-contact with the man but failed at every attempt. She gathered some courage and remembered her authority in the state. "May I know what is happening, Mr. Jamwal?" she asked, looking away. The man smiled and looked away, took out a cell phone from his pocket, and checked something completely irrelevant to the current situation. He then said, "Perhaps it is in everyone's best interest that you do not know."

Mufti now looked at him, her eyes burning in anger that was well-hidden under her calm demeanour. "I would ask you to leave my way. I am heading to the office for some urgent work. Excuse me," she said as she motioned her security staff to proceed with their duty. Jamwal stood there, smiling. Mufti's staff, however, did not budge. They were unaware of the situation but understood the gravity of it all.

"*Murkhaan*, that car will not drive itself. Get going now," Mufti shouted. The driver first saw Mufti's volcanic face, then at the 150+ strong men with automatic assault rifles. It took him a couple of seconds to act against his previous loyalty. Mufti's eyes grew larger and red, her face was red with anger, dying to burst out on the daring disobedience of her direct orders.

"Calm down, Ms. Mufti," Jamwal said. "Worry not. Give your staff a day-off. I'll drop you at your work. Sounds good?" The lady refrained from looking at the man anymore.

"I'll drive myself. Now please ask your men to clear away," she said in a fiery tone.

The smile from Jamwal's face flew instantly. He was being playful, but not anymore. He looked right into her eyes. For a fraction of a second, Nafeesa thought he looked like a madman. "Where are we going anyway? To supervise the stone-pelting yourself or to set some houses on fire and rant to the media about how Indian forces are suppressing the locals? Tell me and I will drop you at the right place in time," he said. Mufti's heart almost skipped a beat.

"*Bakwaas*(rubbish)," she protested. "You can't stop me from serving my office. You are challenging the CM of this state," she challenged Vineet Jamwal.

"Drop the act, lady. Your beloved Dilshad sent us here. He is being 'treated' as a guest in the BSF head-quarter. You mind the same 'homely' treatment," he said in a harsh, firm voice brimming with anger.

Mufti stared at him.

"In the interest of the people of Jammu and Kashmir, you are under house arrest. Your powers at the Chief Minister of the state are on hold until further notice," Jamwal said. "Now if you may please," he said, motioning Nafeesa to get back into the house. "I am inviting myself in for a non-violent cup of coffee, haha," he said with a snarling sarcasm.

***

Jamwal sat in the CM House's beautiful ornamental garden, sipping on the fine cup of Kashmiri *Kahwa* the next morning. He asked one of the house's staff members to keep an eye on Nafeesa

Mufti every fifteen minutes. The premise was heavily guarded and no media-attaché was allowed in the proximity. Jamwal called to his other officers in the state executing an unanticipated plan by the Indian Government.

"Hello. Jai Hind, Malik. How is your sector doing?" Jamwal asked over the satellite phone.

"Till now, everything is fine, sir. I heard about a little disturbance in the lower sector of *Punch* area," Aman Malik said.

"Internal or external reactors?"

"Not known, sir."

"Okay. Keep me updated. 20,000 more Troops are coming in today," he said.

"Yes, sir. I just hope we don't have to use them anyway," Malik said.

"Haha. Let's hope it turns out to be a fine holiday for them too. I'll check on the area you told me about. Lower *Punch*, right?"

"Absolutely, sir."

As soon as the call ended, one of the staff members came running to Jamwal. "*Saheb, saheb,*" his voice shivered. "Yes, what is it?" Jamwal asked. "Bibi is not opening her door. She has locked herself in. There has been no sound inside for the past hour," he informed. "She must be asleep," Jamwal said. "I don't know. She never sleeps at this hour. Something is wrong," the man said frantically.

Jamwal took only a second to order one of his officers and a Jawan to break the door open. The men found Nafeesa lying on the floor. "*Allah,* what happened?" one of her domestic help cried. "Stay quiet," the office said. It was in an instant that Jamwal, post investigating for Mufti's vitals, concluded that she was faking a medical urgency.

"Ravi, call a team of doctors, just in case," Jamwal said, and he left with a small team in an armoured vehicle towards Lower *Punch.*

*****

Lower Punch was as silent as to any other part of the city at that moment. Only a few Mi-17 choppers marked their presence while flying by, or the occasional coos of the native birds broke the silence once in a while. Four of the jawans stepped out of the vehicle and stood guard in a protective stance for the Indian NSA.

The central government had enforced a curfew the last day. Jamwal looked around in the old houses. Nothing much was worth looking at except for a few peeping eyes and heads in the distance. A few shops that retailed medicine and items of daily needs were open. At every intersection, a police jeep stood guard. No more than three people were allowed to walk together in public places. Every inhabitant of the area was instructed to carry an ID at all times. Jamwal turned towards the valley and looked beyond the trees. Down the slope on which one could climb up or down with little difficulty stood wild pine trees. The NSA stepped down the slope.

"Look around and tell if you see something unusual," he instructed the *Jawans.*

A few minutes of sharp and keen search revealed the most probable cause of disturbance that occurred last night. "Here, see this?" Jamwal walked up the slope, a little out of breath, with a piece of a mortar shell. "It came from that side," he said, pointing to the other side of the wide valley, the region that belonged to Pakistan.

"There might be insurgents close by. Ask the CO of this area to man the machine-guns at these points along the ridge. Also, ask them to thoroughly search the houses of suspicious people in this area. Someone must have alerted the other side of possible movement in the region. They wanted to create a nuisance," he said, throwing away the shell.

Jamwal thought of something and stayed back in the *Lower Punch* area. "You guys go ahead. Stay sharp. I'll be here," he said. "Sir, we can't leave you unsecured," one of the senior personnel raised his concern. "I'll be fine, *Bhatt Ji*," he said. "Just want to explore the devil that hides in the details. That can be done here only. Please, go ahead," Jamwal said.

The armoured vehicle roared and stormed back to the CM's House.

Breathing in the fresh air, Jamwal glanced at his wristwatch. 'Almost done,' he thought to himself. He then walked towards a police vehicle some 100 meters from his position. Close to the vehicle parked at the intersection where two roads crossed each other was a daily needs shop and a road-side vendor who was selling tea, omelet, and cigarettes. As Jamwal marched towards the vehicle, the officers recognized him and saluted.

"How is the post...?" Jamwal read the inspector's batch, "Inspector Singh? How is everything?"

"Uh, sir. We had light shelling last night from across the valley. That's the news," Inspector Singh reported.

"The people?"

"Mostly inside. A few roam in the evenings to gather the essential supplies. Not much movement by the civilians, sir."

"Ok," said the NSA as he went to the roadside vendor. The inspector hurried behind him to assist.

"Jai Hind. Give me a cigarette," Jamwal said to the vendor. His long-white beard touched his potbelly, eyes resembled a teenager wanting to explore the world, and the body just shy of 60-odd years. At once, he took out a packet of Dunhill. "Thanks. Make me a sandwich too, *Miya*," Jamwal said. "Would you guys like to have something," he asked the Inspector and his team. Nay, they replied.

NSA Jamwal closely looked at the old vendor as he hustled his way through the utensils, pouring tea from the pots, and finding the cigarette pack from a cloth bag. The old tea-seller took out two freshly baked slices of bread and shaved their hard edges with a shiny big knife. He placed the two slices alongside on a marble slab, cut out four juicy slices of cucumber, sliced a succulent tomato, and placed them atop one slice. The old man coronated the other slice with a slice of cheese and the most beautiful half-fried egg. The two loaded slices were married and grilled for a few seconds before they landed on the plate.

Vineet Jamwal was trying to find calm in the very process of sandwich-making. The plain skill with which the old man did it was amazing and absurdly soothing.

As he stubbed the cigarette under his shoe and devoured the first bite, his mind felt at ease. "*Shukraan, Miyan*," he expressed his gratitude to the old man. "How long have you been working here, *Miyan?*" he asked.

"25-Years," the old man replied. "I came here as a refugee. This land accepted me. I have been living here since and wish to take my last breath here only," the man said with a heavy throat.

"Why do you say so, *Miya*? And, may I know your name? I am Vineet."

"Haji Sadatulla is my name," the old man signalled to end the conversation. The talk almost died when the old man turned-on his old radio set that was able to catch broken pieces from the broadcast.

The shopkeeper who ran the daily-needs store was listening to the short-lived conversation. "Everyone wants to come here. Everyone wants to die here," the man taunted without pointing at anyone. "Huh?" Jamwal was perplexed for a moment.

"You were saying something?" he urged the man to talk more. "This is a beautiful Kashmir. Everyone wants a part of it. 'These' men from across the border, and the Indian government who understands nothing," the shopkeeper said. His cynical words almost hit Jamwal who refrained from giving any explanation.

The old vendor's radio suddenly caught a distorted broadcast- *The Union Government has announced...Article 370 Abrogated... Kashmir...Indian Constitution...Enforced...Citizens rights...Historical move...End of terrorism and suppression...Breaking news.*

The shopkeeper looked at the radio, perplexed. Jamwal and the inspector smiled.

Jamwal stepped towards the shop's counter, asked for a sweet. The shopkeeper handed him the sweet. "200 Rupees," he said. Jamwal gave him the money and offered the sweet to the shopkeeper and the sandwich-maker. "What is this for, *Miyan*?"

the feeble yet bright Sadatulla asked Jamwal as he cleaned his small stall. Jamwal looked at the shopkeeper while speaking to the old man. "Article 370 has been abrogated. Jammu and Kashmir is free now. Every resident of the state will now have the rights of an Indian citizen…" he spoke as he marched back to the police jeep.

Long live my nation

Jai Hind

About the Authors

Vikas Trivedi is from lake city Udaipur in Rajasthan. He pursued and achieved a master's degree in individual streams of English literature, Psychology, and Political Science, and a Ph.D.in Psychology. He now uses his knowledge and education to teach as a professor of psychology and literature.

Vikas used his knowledge of psychology and the laws of attraction to transform his life and overcome problems, both big and small. His belief in the Universe's power and the results he achieved led to a very interesting phase in his life.

The successful duo together had published their second book, '42 Days of Love', which is inspired by the real-life heroics of an Australian deep-sea diver.

Ms. Smita Agarwal hails from Kolkata, West Bengal. As a child, her interests always steered away from academic studies and into creative art. She pursued honours in accountancy and after having graduated, she gave in to her passion for creative work. She ventured into the field of interior designing and received a diploma in computer-aided designing.

Smita also is an extremely knowledgeable and successful Pranic healer, an art she has been practicing for over 13 years. The continual study of Pranic healing is what led her into exploring the powers of the mind, and finally meeting Vikas Trivedi, the two of whom together wrote their debut book 'The Hidden Spark', which became a phenomenon. It received acclaim across India and abroad, and was featured in multiple media channels and newspapers.

Now, their third book is on the facts about '14/2 The Attack on Pulwama' which is based on real incident.